84165174

CALL ME KATE

Meeting the Molly Maguires

MOLLY ROE

Tribute Books
Archbald, Pennsylvania

Tribute Books
PO Box 95, Archbald, PA 18403
Visit our web site at www.tribute-books.com

First Paperback Edition: November 2008
First Hardcover Edition: November 2008

Roe, Molly,
Call Me Kate: Meeting the Molly Maguires
by Molly Roe. – 1st ed.

Summary: Coming of age amidst the seething unrest of the Civil
War era, feisty fourteen-year-old Katie McCafferty infiltrates the
Molly Maguires, a secret Irish organization, to rescue a lifelong
friend. Under the guise of "Dominick," a draft resister, Katie
volunteers for a dangerous mission in hopes of preventing
bloodshed. Katie risks job, family, and ultimately her very life to
intervene. A series of tragedies challenge Katie's strength and
ingenuity, and she faces a crisis of conscience. Can she balance
her sense of justice with the law?

ISBN 978-0-9814619-5-3 / LCCN: 2008940950 (Hardcover)
ISBN 978-0-9814619-3-9 (Paperback)

Printed in the United States of America

Dedicated to my wonderful aunt, Margaret Bonner,
family memory keeper and my biggest fan.
Margie's vivid family stories inspired this book
and kept our ancestors alive for another generation.

ॐ ॐ

Each person dies three times.
First, there is the moment
when the physical body stops functioning.
Second is the time
when the earthly remains are consigned to the grave,
never more to be seen.
Third, there is that moment,
sometime in the future,
in which the person's name is spoken for the last time.
That's when the person is really gone.

Mexican saying

CONTENTS

❧ ❧

PRAISE FOR *CALL ME KATE*

The writing style employed in the book entertains, educates and communicates to the reader a general understanding of the hardships of life in the anthracite coal fields of northeast Pennsylvania in the nineteenth century and Irish-American history.

- Bill Strassner
Museum Educator
Eckley Miners' Village
Weatherly, Pennsylvania
www.eckleyminers.org

Call Me Kate absorbs the reader into a tightly woven narrative of tumultuous times in the anthracite region. Through *Kate,* the reader becomes a participant in that story.

- Ruth Cummings
Museum Educator
Pennsylvania Anthracite Heritage Museum
Scranton, Pennsylvania
www.anthracitemuseum.org

The Lackawanna Historical Society is always pleased to see new and creative ways to promote an interest in our local history. A young adult historical fiction like *Call Me Kate* is a wonderful example of this! We are delighted to know that local authors are using their heritage to develop new publications.

- Mary Ann Moran-Savakinus
Executive Director
Lackawanna Historical Society
Scranton, Pennsylvania
www.lackawannahistory.org

READER COMMENTS

Call Me Kate is the absorbing story of young Kate McCafferty, caught in the struggle between the Irish miners and the cold-hearted mine owners who use them up and throw them away. Set in the tumultuous period of the Civil War, the plucky Kate must find a way to stop the terrible bloodshed threatening her people, the miners of the Patch. Kudos to the author whose meticulous research has made this slice of history come alive!

- H. Morgan

Roe's considerable skill as a storyteller brings this important time alive for the next generation.

- K. Williams

By way of skillful storytelling and rigorous research, (the author) has infused the saga of Kate's everyday life in early coal mining days with the history of a forsaken people and their tragic times. Kate proved herself a mighty heroine. Great reading!

- M. Bonner

Call Me Kate has an authenticity that only comes from personal knowledge of the tumultuous times that gripped the coal mining country and its coal-dust blackened denizens in their struggle... Bravo!

- M. Robinson

Katie McCafferty is an unlikely heroine who will steal your heart. Rising from family tragedy and poverty with determination and spunk, she sees the world of the 1860s as a place of rights and wrongs and chooses a dangerous path of loyalty to her friends and to her own conscience.

- Ann Vitale

INTRODUCTION

The tensions of the Civil War era, a turbulent time in American history, pitted immigrants against nativists, management against labor, and pro-slavery factions against abolitionists. In many northern states, support for the war was weak. President Lincoln had to draft soldiers to fight.

When the Northern draft was enacted in October of 1862, resistance built up in regions where the common people's interests were in jeopardy. Riots broke out in several states, including Pennsylvania. The coal region and farmlands were hotbeds of resistance since losing a breadwinner threatened the survival of the family. The outbreaks of hostility in Pennsylvania were not as large or as violent as the ill-famed New York riot of 1863, but they highlight the lack of northern unity regarding the war. The slogan "rich man's war, poor man's fight" became popular among the masses.

Immigrants resented the hostile reception they received from the Know Nothing Party and other nativist groups who opposed the influx of workers from Europe. At the same time, the country was experiencing a surge of growth in industry and needed cheap labor to mine coal for the production of steel for railroads and other businesses.

Northeastern Pennsylvania had a particularly high percentage of immigrant workers. Irishmen who were recruited for mine work were usually poor unskilled laborers, not certified miners who commanded a higher wage. They performed strenuous and dangerous tasks and were paid by the miner from his earnings. The cultural and religious differences between English and Welsh bosses and Irish and German workers worsened already strained labor relations.

Pay was based on filling coal cars with good clean anthracite, so important safety considerations, like shoring up the roof and clearing rubble, were often neglected in order to fill the cars. Colliery owners were known to pay workers in scrip which could only be used at the Company store, limiting their buying power and their independence.

Mine workers suffered when there were strikes or stoppages, but also when overproduction caused the price of anthracite to drop. Work injuries and deaths were common, and without public welfare agencies, the families had to rely on themselves, their churches, and their benevolent societies. The draft was a flame set to the tinderbox that was the coal region in 1862.

Benjamin Bannan, editor of *The Miners Journal* of Pottsville and Schuylkill County draft commissioner during the Civil War, blamed the "Molly Maguires" for voter fraud, political defeats, the draft riots, violence at the mines, and murders. He contributed to the anti-Irish hysteria of the era by associating the Molly Maguires with the Ancient Order of Hibernians, a benevolent association.

While Katie's adventures are fictional, the events of *Call Me Kate* depict the common experience of those turbulent days.

CHAPTER 1

Coal Mining Crisis – November 1860

"S'ter, s'ter, I need to see Katie right away!" The disheveled boy who burst into our classroom was my friend and former classmate, Con Gallagher. He bent to catch his breath beside the well-polished teacher's desk.

Twenty pairs of horror-filled eyes turned in my direction, then darted back toward the frowning nun, expecting the worst. Sister Mary Charles never tolerated disruptions, especially to her beloved literature class. I was in for it unless Con had a darn good reason to be here.

Ink splashed from the inkwell as I jumped up from my desk, but Sister was even faster. Accompanied by the rattle of rosary beads, she dragged Con into the corridor by a sooty sleeve and told me to return to my seat. I hesitated, then plopped back down. What in the world was happening?

My friend Annie leaned across the aisle and whispered, "This better not be one of Con's pranks or you'll both get paddled."

"Shhh!" Everyone strained to hear the conversation in the hall, but whatever was said did not take long.

"Miss McCafferty, go to the cloakroom and get your belongings please." Sister Mary Charles's no-nonsense voice was tinged with kindness, usually reserved for the Latin scholars.

Since I expected a scolding, Sister's concerned tone bewildered me completely. As I stepped forward, the piercing breaker whistle split the air. A mine accident!

The frightening sound spurred chaotic movement. Girls hugged each other and cried, then one by one my classmates slid to their knees. My whirling thoughts fixed on a terrifying conclusion. Please God, no. Please no.

I ran into the hallway without stopping for my shawl and screamed, "Con, what happened?"

Con caught me by the elbows. His blue eyes met mine. "The coal face your father was working collapsed. His legs are pinned. But he's alive, Katie!"

I broke from his grasp and dashed out of the schoolhouse into the cold gray November morning, a day as bleak as Con's news.

"Does my mother know?" Strands of my unruly auburn hair escaped its pins and stuck to my tear-dampened cheeks. I rubbed it back with my palms.

"Bad news travels fast. She may have run to the scene already, I don't know. I went right to school to tell you to get home."

"HOME? I'm going to the mine!"

"No Katie, go to your house. Someone needs to be there. Dinny went to get Gram and her remedy kit so she'll be set to treat your da' when he arrives. I'll help you tear cloth for bandages and boil the water that Gram will need to clean your father's wounds. Your da' may even be home by now." Con's words made sense so I bolted down the alley, a shortcut to the house.

As we reached the side porch, I heard a measured clopping sound echo down Front Street. My heart clenched and missed a beat. The hoofbeats of the Black Mariah, that omen of misery and death, was headed to the mine. Panic flooded through my veins.

There was no sign of life at our house. I opened the back door and called for my mother. Hollow silence met my call. Down the cellar!

I ran out to the rear of the house while Con went to check with the neighbors. When I lifted the heavy door to the storm cellar, I heard Mother singing a cheerful tune as she sealed jelly jars in a pot of boiling water. She looked up, startled, as I dashed down the steps.

"Katie, what're you doing home before lunch?"

"Didn't you hear the whistle? Hurry, Father's injured!"

The surprise on her face turned to horror. She ran up the stairs, using her apron to wipe her steam-flushed brow as she raced outside. "How do you know?"

"Con came to school to tell me. Father's pinned in the chamber. The men are clearing the entrance to free him."

"Oh God, oh God!" My mother wrung her hands and looked helpless.

I ran inside and got mother's woolen shawl and my old cape. By the time I returned, Con was there, reassuring her that help was coming. "My grandmother is on the way in case her skills are needed."

Con had left before anyone knew how bad Father's injuries were, but the huge fall of rock had killed Johnnie Pat, the young nipper working the doors.

Mother and I set off for the colliery. Con didn't argue this time. He offered to stay behind to read' up for his grandmother. Mrs. Gallagher was a stickler for cleanliness, and her sickbed requirements were well known to Con and his brother Dinny.

A huge crowd had gathered at the mine entrance. Friends rushed up and offered sympathy and news. I turned my back on the large black coach and dark horses hitched nearby. The gloomy-looking Black Mariah reminded me of a large crow hovering over a dying rabbit.

Mother composed her face and stiffened her spine as she came to grips with the situation. I tried to imitate her restraint, even though I felt like sobbing. Our outward courage was shattered an hour later when an ear-piercing scream tore through the crowd.

Johnnie Pat's mother saw her son's body carried out on a litter. He was covered from neck down with sailcloth, but blood from his saturated shirt had seeped through the canvas, and smudge marks marred his still, marble-white face. The younger children, clinging to Mrs. McFadden's skirts, began to howl, echoing their mother's cry. She collapsed next to the litter, sobbing bitterly. Her elderly father comforted her, then turned to beckon to our parish priest.

Father Maloney, wearing a violet stole over his black cassock, anointed Johnnie's forehead while intoning in Latin "Si es capax." If thou art alive. No one here had any doubt that Johnnie was dead.

I automatically translated the Latin prayer. Through this holy unction may the Lord pardon thee of whatever sins or faults thou hast committed. Johnnie's faults were minor - quarreling with his older sister, teasing his little brothers, maybe pocketing a few mints from the barrel at the Company store. Johnnie Pat had been in my younger sister's class until he went to work in the mines. If God is just, then Johnnie's place in Heaven will be higher than the biggest boss's here on Earth. Where would the owners stand on Judgment Day?

The women of the Patch surrounded the boy's heartbroken mother. They cared for the other McFadden children while their brother's body was whisked away. In the Patch, giving comfort to the grief stricken was a well-cultivated skill.

I held my mother's elbow to steady her as Father was brought out. Although he was alert, no one knew just how serious his injuries were. The priest once again stepped forward, this time to perform the last rites in full. Father clasped a crucifix while the priest anointed his eyelids, ears, nostrils, lips, hands, and feet. Mother moaned once, then bit her clenched fist to keep from sobbing.

After the blessing, the company men carried Father to the waiting coach. Mother and I kept pace alongside as best we could, but fell behind the horse-drawn vehicle on the steep incline of Ridge Street. I was glad Con had stayed behind to wait.

By the time we reached the house, the workers had taken Father from the tall black carriage and lowered his mangled body onto the splintery porch floorboards. Mother choked back a cry at the sight of his gray, pain-filled face and awkwardly twisted torso. She knelt and caressed his bruised hand.

"Here's Gram," said Con, leaping the bannister to help the white-haired woman who trudged across our yard carrying a bundle. Old Mrs. Gallagher, Con and Dinny's grandmother, was renowned as a healer and herbalist. Her daughter-in-law, Deirdre, was right behind her, toting a large satchel. Dinny, Con Gallagher's identical twin, arrived with a basket of supplies as the workers hurried off to deliver the next accident victim to his grieving family. Directions flew as the old woman went into action.

"Dinny, go over street and get Catharine McCall and Aggie McCafferty." Dinny dashed off to get my grandmother and great-aunt who lived across town.

"Con and Katie, take hold of one side of this sheet and help lift Jack. Deirdre, you and Mary take the other side. Careful now!"

We shuffled our way into the parlor and placed Father on a pallet on the floor. Mrs. Gallagher opened her bag and took out several items.

"Katie, I need soap and water, and clean rags."

Quickly cutting off Father's shredded pants legs, she expertly removed scraps of fabric and embedded coal from the wound, then pressed it to stop the bleeding.

As she began sewing up the wounds, I frowned, sensing something strange. Father was not screaming with pain. He did not wince at the cleaning of the wounds or stitching of his flesh. Mrs. Gallagher shook her head and glared at me when I opened my mouth.

"Katie, take these soiled rags to the burner and bring fresh." She shoved a bowl of blood- drenched cloth at me with a meaningful look. I scrambled to obey, but by the time I returned the procedure was finished.

"Rest and quiet are what Jack needs now. Go on, all of yeh, and let him sleep off the shock."

Deirdre and my mother began cleaning the parlor while Mrs. Gallagher lifted Father's head to give him sips of willow tea. Con and I went out on the porch where I asked the questions that were pounding inside my head.

"Tell me how the accident happened. Were you right there? Who else was hurt?"

"Hold on, Katie. Calm down. I'll tell you what I know, if you're sure you're ready to hear it."

I inhaled deeply and sat on the railing, hugging the post. "Tell me."

"I was outside in the gangway loading coal while Sam Davison and his buttie were in the chamber preparing to blast the coalface. Your father had just taken a hand augur into the room for Sam to drill a hole for the powder when there was the creaking sound of a squeeze. I only had time to cover my head and crouch. It was pure luck that the coal car protected me from the shower of rock." Con shook his head at his miraculous escape.

"Poor Johnnie Pat wasn't lucky. He only started as door keeper last month, and he didn't recognize the warning sounds. The rock slide shattered the beams, and Johnnie was hit by a flying splinter." Con stopped and rubbed his forehead, screening his eyes from my sight before continuing.

"When I heard him scream, I ran to help, but the stake was lodged solid in his chest. I couldn't do anything but pillow his head with my jacket." Con's voice cracked. "The poor lad cried out 'Mama! Mama!'... then he died in my arms." Con hid his face in the crook of his elbow.

"I'm so sorry for making you relive the horror, Con. Please forgive me."

"No, I want to tell what happened." Back in control, Con recounted the rest in a near monotone. Once started, he seemed incapable of stopping his recitation.

"I yelled into the blocked chamber and your father answered. He, Sam, and Packy were all injured. The only entry was blocked so I couldn't get to them."

"Thank God they weren't suffocated," I said. "Why aren't there two exits?"

"We've been trying to convince the owners that there should always be two shafts sunk every time a new mine is opened, but they say the cost is too great."

My sorrow simmered into rage at the operators' neglect.

"When the rescuers came to free the men, I ran to school to get you."

"Oh no, Sarah and Maymie! No one went to their classroom."

"It's better that your sisters stay in school until your mother is settled and your grandmother's here. Maymie, especially, is too young to help, and she'd be horrified by the blood. Thank God she didn't see Johnnie as we saw him today."

That day permanently changed our lives. Father's wounds healed, but he did not regain use of his legs. Everyone in the family assumed new chores, and a feeling of insecurity fell upon us. Then the Christmas season arrived, and the busyness of the holidays helped take our minds off the future. The money that Sarah, Maymie and I had saved to buy candy and small gifts for each other was put toward the household accounts, but no one complained. The best Christmas gift was that Father was still with us.

Our family income was at its lowest point. Father had been earning only part-time wages since late spring. The mines had just started up full time for the winter heating season when the tragedy occurred.

We sold Father's tools and made a tidy sum, but much of the money went toward medical needs. Our family buckled down and made cuts in the budget.

December 1860 was a time of change for the whole country, not just our family. Distant events would have far-reaching consequences for almost everyone in the Patch.

The week before Christmas, my mother and I ran into Annie O'Donnell and her family at the Company Store. Annie and I were whispering about the handsome stock boy when the tone of our mothers' conversation caught our attention. Mrs. O'Donnell held a newspaper with a banner headline that read, "The Union Dissolved."

My mother frowned and said, "South Carolina has finally broken away?"

"Yes, Lincoln's election gave South Carolina the reason it was looking for." Mrs. O'Donnell looked disgusted. "This will mean war. President Buchanan will have to defend federal property in South Carolina."

"Why do they want to leave the Union?" asked Annie.

"They've been threatening for years now, but the election of Lincoln set a flame to the slavery issue," sighed Mother.

"At least South Carolina is far away," I said.

Mrs. O'Donnell declared, "Not far enough. Even though no shots have been fired, my boys are already talking about going off to soldier."

CHAPTER 2

Company's Coming – March 1861

"Catharine Agnes McCafferty, get off that culm bank and come in here. Now!" Grammam McCall's voice bellowed from the kitchen window.

"Ah, drat." The early March day was sunny and mild, and I hated to miss the games that my friends, Dinny and Con, had organized. Mine holidays were rare, but today the whole country was celebrating the inauguration of our new president, Honest Abe Lincoln.

It was fun competing against the boys who were usually working in the mines, but I knew that when Grammam used my full name, she meant business.

I reluctantly clambered from my perch as king of the hill, and skittered down the last few feet of the bank in a cloud of sooty coal dust. I brushed the black powder from my hem while trying to ignore the taunts of "Aaagggie, yer mother's callin'." Dinny shouted a few rude comments before turning back to the game.

"Ah, cork it, you blatherskite, or you'll be sorry when I get back." I yelled toward the patched britches scrambling back up the heap.

My smudgy gingham dress was hiked above my ankles in a way which always annoyed my relatives. I didn't purposely provoke my mother and grandmother, but it was impossible to stay clean and neatly dressed with so many opportunities to romp with the other children of Murphy's Patch. The looming culm bank behind our house was only one temptation. The woods and tumbling streams on the south side also beckoned to my adventurous spirit.

The Patch, tucked in the eastern Pennsylvania mountains, looked unappealing to outsiders, but my friends and I enjoyed its limitless possibilities: building tree houses, racing homemade sailboats in Panther Creek, and swinging into the lake on the far side of Hauto Mountain on a sling made of scraps salvaged from the colliery. If Gram and Aunt Aggie heard about my adventures, I'm sure they'd advise my parents to send me away to a convent.

By the time I reached our lane, I was breathless, but I swished my skirt with a snap, stomped the dirt from my high-laced brogans, and bounded through the door. Standing on a sturdy dooley box at the wash sink was my younger sister Sarah, scouring a heavy iron skillet. Gram stood near the kitchen table where pounds of potatoes lay unpeeled.

"How can yeh be so feckless, goin' off on a lark while Sarah's stuck here doing all of yer chores? I've never seen the beat of yeh," Gram sputtered.

I lowered my head and muttered, "Sorry, Grammam."

"Y'know yer poor mother's in a state, worryin' about yer father since his accident. She's exhausted from struggling to make ends meet, baking and putting up preserves to sell."

"Yes, M'am."

"Can't you act like a well-behaved young lass instead of a hooligan? Now look at the condition of yer clothes! Hurry to the pump and wash up, put on your shawl, and wait on the porch for yer mother."

"Where did Mother go?"

"She's at the Company Store buyin' baking soda for this

week's bread orders. She'll be back any minute, and she'll be wantin' to ask yeh somethin'."

I tried to escape Gram's scolding, but couldn't avoid her final pointed remarks.

"And do something about that wild mop of hair!"

With an apologetic look at my sister, I went to do as Grammam asked. It was bad luck that Gram came across the yards and found Sarah doing my job. I knew my pious sister was upset at being caught up in my dishonesty. I mentally promised to give Sarah my new plaid hair ribbon.

Sarah, Maymie, and I were very different. Neither of my two sisters angered the old biddies the way I seemed to do. Gram hinted that I was a changeling that the fairies put in the McCafferty cradle.

Gram's stories about fairies, leprechauns and changelings entertained us on long winter evenings. Many of the tales were amusing, but Gram, Aunt Aggie and Old Mrs. Gallagher also told bloodchilling stories. The Coach-a-Bower sounded like the Black Mariah, except that it was driven by a headless driver! The tales of the other world prickled my arms with goosebumps, especially since I knew the women believed every word they uttered.

The old ones warned my sisters and me to leave tokens out for the fairies, and to listen for the banshee's cry. I often thought that if there were fairies, they wouldn't bother seeking us here in Pennsylvania. After all, why would they leave Ireland and their fragrant blackthorn trees and buried gold to come here where the only thing to dig up was lumpy black coal?

I splashed cold water on my face, tidied up, then bounced onto the sturdy wooden swing Father made before the mine accident. Everything was fine before that dark November day. The memory of the piercing mine whistle was seared into my mind. The entire Patch had rallied to help our family, but even with everyone's assistance it had been an uphill battle.

I clenched my fists in frustration. If only I'd been born a boy! Then I could take father's place as breadwinner. At fourteen, I could work as a mule driver with a long whip and earn almost as much as a grown man. My friends, Dinny and Con, had earned money as nippers and breaker boys since they were nine.

I would've been named John Patrick, after my grandfather, instead of Catharine Agnes. Then I wouldn't have had to suffer from taunts likening me to the dreadful Aunt Aggie. When I wasn't compared to my bossy great-aunt, I was contrasted with my two younger sisters, Sarah and Maymie. "They're ladylike girls," the old biddies always informed me. Neither of my sisters ever got in trouble in school, and both were fastidious in their dress. At least they weren't tattletales, or I'd really be in trouble at home.

My unruly red hair betokened my personality, according to our teacher, Sister Mary Charles. Maybe she was right. Or maybe I was just accident prone. One day while playing hide-and-seek at recess, Annie O'Donnell and I accidentally toppled a life-size statue from the grotto onto the grass. Luckily the Madonna wasn't damaged, but all our efforts could not replace her on the pedestal before the nuns arrived to march us back to class. Everyone kept mum through the afternoon of interrogations that followed. Children in the Patch learned from an early age that there was nothing worse than a squealer.

A murmur of voices interrupted my wandering thoughts. I spragged my feet to halt the swing and craned my neck to see past the porch post. Mother and Mr. Breslin, the fire boss at the mine, chatted as they approached the house.

Breslin was a bachelor, so I supposed he was here to buy some of Mother's delicious baked goods. He was pretty old, at least 30, but since his mam had passed away, I guessed he needed looking after. We certainly needed the extra money - if that was why he came. Every little bit counts, Mother always said.

I wondered if his visit was the reason Gram told me to freshen up. An uncomfortable notion entered my mind seeing them stroll down the path, especially since Grammam said Mother had something important to ask me. The uneasy feeling grew stronger as I remembered the hushed conversation I'd interrupted on the porch last night. As soon as I'd crossed the door sill, the older women switched to Irish so I couldn't understand the conversation. Putting two and two together, I entertained a truly horrible idea. My stomach started to churn ... they were arranging a marriage behind my back! Glory be, not that old man!

My face blazed scarlet with temper, and my mother eyed me with concern as she stepped onto the porch in front of Mr. Breslin. My disposition was considered unpredictable.

"Hello, Katie darling, I'm sure you remember Mr. Breslin who was so good to your father after the accident." I grudgingly bobbed a curtsy in respect for his support, but I was only willing to go so far for kindness sake!

"I'm glad you're here, Katie," Mother continued, "because Mr. Breslin and I have an idea we want to put to you." Oh Lord, it's true. The churning turned into a knot of dread in my stomach.

"You'll remember that Mrs. Breslin, God rest her soul, was laid to rest last month."

We nodded our heads to acknowledge the memory. It had been a fine wake and funeral, for Mrs. Breslin was one of the oldest residents of the Patch, and her son was respected for his position in the Company. Everyone able to walk followed the hearse to the new cemetery on Big Mine Hill.

"I'm sorry for your trouble, Mr. Breslin, but we know she's in a better place," I said. Now that the formalities were satisfied, I chafed to find out if my suspicions were true.

"Well, these past few months Mr. Breslin had to cook and clean for himself. That is where you fit in." Oh, no, here it comes!

Panic-stricken, and needing to delay the terrible moment, I blurted out, "I'm sure there are at least five women in the Patch who'd have you, Mr. Breslin. Miss Cannon up in Storm Hill has been waiting at least ten years to wed. Were you wanting me to see if I can make you a match?" A stunned silence greeted my offer. Mother looked as if she wished the ground would swallow up her outrageous daughter.

"That is NOT what we had in mind, Catharine Agnes. Father Maloney recommended you as a domestic until Mr. Breslin's widowed sister arrives to keep house."

"A job as Mr. Breslin's servant? A domestic job at your house?" I turned from one to the other with a confused, embarrassed face even rosier than before. Whissht! I sighed with relief as the millstone lifted off my shoulders. I was not being married off to save the family. "Thank you, thank you! I accept the position. That is, if you are still offering it to me."

"Yes, Katie, the job is yours," said Mr. Breslin in a firm voice. "Although when I arrived I thought maybe the good Father had the wrong girl in mind. You didn't look like the pleasant, quick-witted, energetic lass he'd described."

"Oh, sorry about that sir, you just surprised me. I thought you came to the house for another reason, ... uh ... to buy my mother's raisin scones!"

CHAPTER 3

Collecting a Salary – March 1861

Hallelujah! I inhaled the spring air and tossed my bonnet into the cloudless sky as I headed home from my last day of school. I trotted down the steep alley that connected the east and west ends of Murphy's Patch.

Our town huddled on the hills east of the Panther Creek Valley so everything was either up or down hill. Patch towns sprouted wherever a coal company started operations. The town grew from a few narrow plank houses that the Company slapped together for the workers, and gradually spread beneath the skeletal shadow of the Number 10 breaker. The original buildings were weathered a uniform gray from dirt and the elements. Some wealthier families whitewashed their homes every spring, but it was difficult to maintain the siding when daily doses of smoke and dust puffed over the town.

Most houses were arranged in a straight line of porch, parlor, living room, and kitchen. People joked that you could throw a clinker from the front step through to the back yard without hitting anything inside.

I liked school, but the job at Mr. Breslin's was a wonderful opportunity to earn a salary and help my family. Laudanum to relieve the worst of Father's pain was one thing my earnings would buy, but medicine was not our only need.

The monthly rent was the most important debt to settle. Otherwise the Lehigh Coal and Navigation Company would turn our home over to a working family. The Company was in business to make money, and the bosses weren't about to let a perfectly good house be used by a family that didn't have a single working man, nor hopes of one.

When Dinny and Con Gallagher's father died, their family was allowed to stay in the company house rent free until the twins were ten, old enough to work at the breaker picking slate. Their last six years' wages went toward the back rent. It was like slavery working off all that debt.

Father learned about my employment plans on the Saturday before I started the job. It was not a pleasant evening.

Mother and I went upstairs after supper to break the news. She stepped into the room and arranged herself on the rocker near the head of the bed. The plan was to approach the matter cautiously.

"It's warm for this time of year, isn't it Jack?"

"'Tis," replied my father.

"Did you enjoy your supper?" she asked.

"Looking for compliments, are yeh?" asked my father with a glint in his eye.

My mother realized there was no use making idle conversation. My father knew something was up.

"Jack, it seems as if our prayers were answered. Hugh Breslin is in dire need of a domestic for general cleaning and laundry, and our Katie fits the bill."

"Mary, love, you know Catharine can't be quitting school and neglecting her education. She's to be the first McCafferty to earn a diploma!"

"She'll only miss a few months of classes, then school will be letting out for the planting season. By late summer, Ellen Malloy will be here to replace Katie as housekeeper. Katie can continue her schooling next year."

"Once Katie starts earning a salary, she'll lose her ambition to study."

I squirmed with impatience, wanting to add my two cents to the conversation, but Mother's firm gaze warned me to remain in the doorway.

"Now Jack, a bright girl like Catharine can study every evening and do school assignments with Sarah and her friends. And you can teach her Latin when you feel up to it. You were ever the classical scholar growing up."

"Don't be giving me that blarney, Mary, I know you're buttering me up! Even your way with words can't make me feel happy about passing our burdens onto Catharine."

"Well, I hate to say this, Jack, but we have no other choice. The Company sent a letter threatening to evict us if we don't pay the rent. My baking money doesn't stretch far enough. I just don't see any alternative."

With brow furrowed and eyes closed, my father pondered this, and then beckoned to me. "Katie, will you promise to finish your education?"

I nodded.

"Remember, knowledge is power. If our people were allowed an education, Ireland wouldn't be in the state it's in."

Father was optimistic that living in America would mean progress for his children. We would never again have to suffer the lack of self-determination that led to the Great Hunger.

Formal education was denied Catholics in Ireland, so my parents had been taught in secret at Irish hedge schools. They were both adept at reading, writing, and the classics, but were weak in math and science.

"Of course I'll get an education. Once we get on our feet again, I'll go back to St. Anne's." After a painful moment of silence, Father gave his final comment.

"Well, what can I say then. God's will be done!" He turned his face away.

Poor Father! We all knew he considered himself a burden on the family. He was disappointed that I was temporarily leaving school, but understood that my salary would take some of the load from Mother's shoulders.

My weekly pay would supplement Mother's baking money and the small sums earned from gathering berries and nuts in season. We McCaffertys were only one step from the Carbon County poorhouse at Laurytown, God save us.

On my first day of work, I arrived at Breslin's house on Ridge Street and was pleasantly surprised that the house was not too disheveled for a bachelor's place. Old Mrs. Breslin had raised my new employer well.

I cleaned downstairs in the morning, cooked dinner at noon, and made an inventory of supplies in the afternoon. Three neighbor women stopped by for a chat when they spotted me on the porch. I learned some tidbits about my employer's family and heard the gossip from the east end of town. That side of the Patch was a lot busier than ours. All the miners streamed down through Goat Town into the Patch looking like the scorched legions of Old Nick marching out of Hell. It startled a person to see the white of their eyes in those smudgy gray faces. When they came out of the wash shanty, the men looked human again.

I packed cold meat, two hard-cooked eggs, a chunk of cheese, and crusty bread in the growler for Mr. Breslin's lunch break. Mining was strenuous work, and the men needed hearty meals. The heavy metal lid of the pail snapped on securely to keep the rats out. Mine rats were extremely clever thieves. Hanging the lunches from the support beams was one way the men protected their meals. Even so, determined rodents figured out how to chew through the strings suspending the lunch pails to devour the scattered food.

Some miners tossed pieces of their sandwiches to the rats since the ends were dirty from their sooty hands anyway. Even though the creatures were bothersome at times, they were also the miners' allies. Many a miner owed his life to watching the behavior of mine rats. When their keen instincts warned them of danger, the rats swarmed to safety in droves. Flooding and roof collapses were only two of the dangers that rats predicted.

At day's end, I cleaned up the dishes and damped the stove, swept the kitchen and porch, and laid out Breslin's nightshirt and wash water. A feeling of accomplishment swept through me. I had even completed a list of chores for the rest of the week.

Too bad Mr. Breslin's sister was coming over from Donegal to care for her brother. I hated the thought of losing such a good position. By my calculations, I'd have about four months of work before Ellen Malloy arrived at Castle Garden in New York City.

Immigrants arrived from Ireland daily, although not as many as when my family arrived in Black '47, the height of the Great Hunger. From the stories the older folks told, at least half the townland of Doochary died during the potato famine, and many others emigrated. The sad letters Gram received from her cousin in the Glenties workhouse cast a melancholy atmosphere over the family members who remembered the Old Sod and a life lost to them forever.

Sarah, Maymie, and I were American citizens, born right here in the heart of Pennsylvania coal country. Father became a naturalized citizen five years ago and so did mother since she was the wife of an American citizen. Gram and Aunt Aggie were the only ones who were still under Queen Victoria's rule, although I've learned to never mention that. The old biddies had never forgiven the English queen for feasting while her Irish subjects starved.

As I entered our lane, Sarah rushed out to greet me. "How'd it go, Katie?"

"Fine, of course. Haven't I been working all my days anyway? It's no different - except for the pay, of course!"

"What is Breslin's house like?"

"The house is in good shape, considering."

"Did you work hard?"

"Now Sarah, you know I'm a hard worker."

"Tell me about your duties."

"I dusted the parlor and dining room and beat the rugs on the first floor. My arms ache from rolling and lifting them on my own."

"I hope you did a good job. We don't want word getting out that the McCaffertys are slapdash about work."

"Don't be such a fussbudget. I won't blacken the family name, for goodness sake."

"What will you do the rest of the week?" My sister was a great one for the questions.

"Hold on. I'm getting to that..." I told my sister about the chores I would do, ending with a plan to fill the larder. "I'll even stock up on some of Aunt Aggie's homemade jellies for a treat. It's a miracle that a sourpuss like Aggie can create such delicious sweets."

"Katie, you shouldn't speak about your elders that way!" said Sarah.

"Oh, don't be so shocked. You know Aunt Aggie is known far and wide for her sharp tongue. Well, Miss Busybody, did I tell you everything you wanted to know?"

"You didn't say if you made dinner," said Sarah.

"Yes, I had a lovely bit of lamb, floury boiled potatoes, and carrots on the table when the noon whistle blew. What with the soda bread I brought from home, it was a meal fit for a king."

"Katie, don't let your success go to your head. Remember, pride goes before a fall," cautioned Sarah.

"Sarah, you goose, I know that every day won't be as wonderful as today, but let me enjoy it while it lasts. Keep preaching and I won't fill you in on the juicy gossip I heard over on Ridge Street today."

With that tantalizing hint, I flipped open the screen door and entered the kitchen. Mother quickly rinsed and dried her hands, then greeted me with a hug.

"So the working lass is home after a long day of toil."

"Oh Mother, I'm so happy I could dance a jig!"

"Well, save your energy so you can tell us all about it after supper. Why don't you go upstairs and sit with your father while Sarah and I lay the table. He'd love to hear about your position and any of the news from over town. Today was a good day, so you can spend a half hour or so in the rocker without disturbing his rest."

I hooked my bonnet and shawl on the peg in the hallway before I ascended the narrow wooden stairs. The creaky company house was not a mansion by any means, but it was our home, and I would hate to lose it. By hook or by crook I was determined my family would not face the disgrace of the poorhouse.

Father was in the front bedroom, entrapped in his feeble body. All hope of regaining use of his legs had been abandoned, but Father accepted his fate with quiet fortitude.

"Macushla, you're a sight for sore eyes! Not many men can claim such a lovely and intelligent daughter. I hope your man Breslin treated you well."

"Yes, Father, so far Mr. Breslin seems to be a grand employer."

"His people are all upstanding folk. 'Tis a pity his father died so young, leaving the care of the children to their mother. The Hunger cut down many a man who sacrificed every bite of potato and shred of bacon so his family wouldn't starve. It's glad I am that all four survived to carry on the Breslin line."

"Yes, and they've done well for themselves, too. Mr.

Breslin's house has some beautiful furnishings, lace curtains, and cabinet portraits of his family. His sister, Annie, works over in Mauch Chunk in the rectory for Father Coffey. And his brother, Daniel, was just promoted to foreman of the Cranberry colliery up the line."

"Indeed, that's a feather in his cap. He's a credit to the Patch. It is about time better jobs are given to hardworking Irishmen. Would that it had happened sooner."

"The labor unrest up north is worsening though, going by what the neighbor ladies say. In Audenried there was a murder. Robert Rhys, one of the bosses, was shot on his way to Silverbrook. Two men were seen running from the scene."

"Aye, I heard about a gang called the Buckshots or the Molly Maguires mentioned more than once in hushed conversations at Cullen's saloon last fall." Father fell silent. Whether he was thinking about the gangs or his own accident I did not know, but either way it was an awkward stillness to break. I vainly tried to think of something cheerful to say. Mother's voice calling me to dinner was a welcome sound.

"Coming, Mother!" I turned back to Father and told him how much he would enjoy the supper mother had prepared to celebrate my first day of work.

"Sarah is worried that all this attention will make me unbearable. She already reminded me that pride is the first of the Seven Deadly Sins, as if I didn't learn that in catechism class two years ago!"

My youngest sister, Maymie, entered the room with a platter covered with a clean tea towel. Savory smells arose from the food as Maymie placed the plate on the well-scrubbed board father used as a bed tray. I helped to settle father comfortably, then went downstairs to the kitchen.

Mother was a magician with budgeting. Tonight she served potatoes whipped with butter and leeks, a lovely slice of ham, and asparagus from the Pennsylvania Dutch farmer. Zern's wagon delivered produce every Monday morning from the farmlands to the south. Dessert was the best part of the meal, sweet bread pudding with a dollop of cream. Ummm, lovely with a hot cup of tea.

During the meal my family assailed me with so many questions that my mind was spinning. The McCaffertys were overwhelming when everyone spoke at once. Even as a member of the opinionated clan, it was hard to keep pace. Strangers found us impossible. Eventually all the female curiosity was satisfied and the good warm food consumed. The family laughed when I retold of the story of the day I got the job. My misplaced concern that Mother was trying to marry me off to Breslin now seemed ridiculous. Later that night, as I knelt against the bed saying an extra prayer of thanksgiving, I realized hope had spread its fluttery wings in our hearts again.

The 12th of April was a sad day for our country. Rebel troops bombarded Fort Sumter. I had not paid much attention when the southern states began to leave the Union because Father's injuries kept us fully occupied. Our day-to-day struggle seemed more important than the political news. But the tentacles of those troubles in the South reached out to ensnare us.

People in the region were very angry at the Southern states. Everyone said that we would whup them in a few weeks.

War kept the mines working full time. Colliery work usually slumped once heating season was over, but now coal was needed to move the troops and supplies. I thought of one of Aunt Aggie's favorite sayings, "Thorny brambles produce fruit in season." So too did the war provide employment for the miners.

By the end of April, the town's army recruits were outfitted for service. On the day of their departure, trumpet notes and drumbeats echoing off the houses beckoned the citizens out to the narrow street to watch our Union troops march to the station. I stood on Breslin's walkway watching our country's proud flag flapping in the breeze. The bright red, white and blue fabric made my heart leap with joy. The young men of the Patch who volunteered to soldier marched proudly in their blue uniforms, singing the John Brown song. I waved to Joe Burns, Miles Shovlin, and other former classmates from St. Anne's in the parade. I placed my right hand over my heart to show the boys my appreciation of their service.

The splendid troops were headed to Baltimore for training and then to battle for three months. Women waved handkerchiefs and men shouted praise to the soldiers. I envied the boys' ability to join up and leave the coal region for such a noble adventure.

CHAPTER 4

Clothesline Calamity

"When, like the dawning day, Eileen Aroon
Love sends his early ray, Eileen Aroon.
What makes his dawning glow
Changeless through joy and woe
Only the constant know..."

I sang some of the words to "Eileen Aroon," and hummed the parts I didn't know while hanging the clean sheets and long-johns on the line. The lyrics about "the dawning day" reminded me that I began this burdensome chore at five o'clock this morning. Thank goodness wash day was only once a week. All down the block, sheets flapped like the sails of masted ships listing on a restless sea. Housewives and maids were busy with the Monday chores after a day of rest.

If the May weather stayed warm and sunny, next week I'd take on the task of washing the lace curtains that graced Breslin's parlor windows. Maybe I'd have pretty things and a home of my own someday. Our family budget had never allowed for decorative furnishings, but our neighbors, the Gallaghers, possessed some lovely items, including crisp lace curtains that I'd always admired.

When I was younger, I enjoyed many afternoons at the

Gallagher homestead where Deirdre and Old Mrs. Gallagher treated me like one of the family. I helped them roll the freshly washed and starched curtains in blotting towels, then carefully snag the lace edges on the needle-like nails that edged the stretcher's wooden frame. Deirdre said I had the nimble fingers needed for such delicate work.

I'd have to remember to borrow Deirdre's stretcher frame to reshape the lace while it dried. I'd also have to order some mild, pleasant-scented savon de marseilles soap from the Company store. Mr. Breslin gave me a budget for ordering necessities. The larder was a bit bare so I'd have to shop for staples like sugar, flour, and dry goods this week. When the farmer's wagon came, I'd get brown eggs and fresh vegetables, too.

Cool droplets from the damp laundry splashed my cheeks, interrupting my wandering thoughts. The spritzing was refreshing on this unusually muggy afternoon. Intense sunlight radiated upon the Patch, quickly drying the fabric. I squinted against the blinding glare of the boraxed linens. Random gusts of warm wind billowed the sheets and tangled them against the clothes prop that held the weight of the bedding aloft. I stood on tiptoe with extra clothes pegs clenched in my teeth and stretched my arms to secure the final items on the worn rope line. Phew! That was the last creaky wicker basket of wet laundry to hang. Most of the moisture had already evaporated from the first clothesline so I started taking down some items to press. The heavy iron was already heating on the stove.

I hoisted the basket onto my hip with aching arms and headed up the wooden steps, thinking how wonderful a cool glass of lemonade would taste. I would empty the tin rinse buckets after a short, well-deserved break.

Just as I grasped the metal handle on the screen door, a terrible din pierced my ears. What in heaven was happening?

The answer materialized as chaos erupted before my eyes. A terrified raccoon which must have wandered from the woods on the south side of town leapt three yards ahead of a mangy pack of mongrels. Every unchained mutt in Murphy's Patch burst through the hedge enclosing Breslin's yard, or so it seemed. Small scrabbling terriers dug through the base of the hedge while some larger bird dogs and hounds hurdled right across the four foot shrubs! The muddy bodies of the dogs showed that the animals had detoured through the Panther Creek before tearing down Ridge Street in a headlong chase.

Disaster erupted before my horrified eyes. The raccoon had noticed a space in the lattice beneath the porch and headed directly toward me. Feeling sympathy for the poor wild creature, I started back down the steps but was alarmed to see the dogs change direction to continue the chase.

The large hound leading the pack had more speed than agility. He lurched against the slanted wooden clothes prop and dislodged it causing the weight of the sheets to crash down on the next few dogs.

Bounding, leaping dogs squirmed under the white linen and tried to rip their way out. The melee gave the masked critter a chance to squirm for cover under the porch. The remaining large dogs set up a howling barkfest, but they could not squeeze under the lattice. Unless stopped, the smaller dogs would eventually reach the huddled raccoon and tear it to pieces. Meanwhile, my lovely sparkling white sheets were being covered with paw prints and muddy splotches from the dirty invaders.

I reached down to retrieve a pillow case, but a small feisty terrier snatched one end and entered into a game of tug of war. As I jerked the cloth away, the determined dog clung on and was lifted a foot off the ground. Feeling ridiculous carrying the dog by his teeth, I lowered the cloth and stomped my feet in frustration. A loud crack sounded, and I whipped my head around. Another clothes prop hit the ground. I gave up on the pillowcase and ran to rescue the laden line that drooped toward the grass.

The entire yard looked like a circus gone wild, with dogs under towels, dragging stockings through the dirt, and chasing each other. I made my way through the obstacle course to the porch looking for a weapon. How could I get rid of these beasts? Eyeing the metal tubs, I was inspired.

In a fury, I lifted the first of two sloshing rinse tubs and heaved the water at the pack. With whimpers and shocked yips, several of them turned tail and ran off. The more stubborn members of the pack needed some shooing with the broom and a second wetting with the extra rinse pail.

Just when I thought I would never get rid of the last few dogs, a dark-haired girl came whooping into the yard, whistling and yelling. They finally retreated after seeing that I had reinforcements.

I looked at the mayhem caused by the nasty brutes and wanted to dissolve into tears. Grass-stained and mud-smeared laundry was everywhere. Three clothes props lay scattered on the ground, and I spotted at least one badly torn sheet. Breslin's long johns now scandalously decorated the iron gate to the street. Hours' worth of work had been undone in five minutes.

A burning wetness filled my eyes and was about to brim over when my unknown helper approached to see if I were injured. Not wanting to seem like a crybaby, I used my apron to press back the tears that were forming. I hoped she would think I was dabbing my sweaty brow.

"Are you alright?"

"Yes, I suppose so. But what a mess!"

"I was on my way home from the store when I saw those dogs run by. I knew trouble would follow. Looks like I made it in time to save Mr. Raccoon's life, but I don't think I helped you much. You were doing a fine job dispersing the mob on your own, I must say."

"Thank you so much. After I threw the last tub of water I didn't know what else I could do. Your yelling surprised them enough to give me the upper hand. Some victory. I still have to clean up the wreckage and start over!"

"My name is Rhianwyn Evans -from across the street. I'll get my sister and we'll help you tidy up the yard,"

"My goodness, you don't even know me and you're offering to help?"

"Tell me your name, and we won't be strangers any more."

"I'm so sorry, my manners have deserted me. I'm Katie McCafferty from the west end. I've been working here as a domestic since March, but my job ends next month when Mr. Breslin's sister arrives. Everything has gone very well until today, but I'll never get this mess cleaned up before Mr. Breslin gets home from his shift at the mine."

"Don't worry. I'll be right back!" Rhianwyn left the yard almost as quickly as she had arrived, and returned moments later accompanied by a taller girl with braided hair.

"Katie, this is Gilys, my older and wiser sister," said Rhianwyn.

"Pleased to meet you, Katie. Looks like you have some work to do. Let's get started so you can get home in time for supper. I'll collect the bedding, Katie, while you boil more water to rewash this laundry. Wynnie, start ironing anything that is still clean. I'll mend the torn sheet." The tall girl certainly took charge quickly, I thought.

"Please call me Wynnie." said the younger sister. "It's the nickname my little brother gave me, and I like it a lot better than Rhianwyn. Oh, and my sister prefers Jill to Gilys."

"I really appreciate your help. I didn't know where to begin."

"Well, you'd better start by getting the long-johns off the gate before Miss Witherby next door sees them and passes out cold. Then you'll have more trouble on your hands!" I laughed imagining the scene, but took her advice.

"Look, over there!" Wynnie pointed to the bristling snout

poking out beneath the porch floorboards. The cautious raccoon checked to see if the murderous group of dogs were gone.

"Oh you miserable creature, go back to the woods where you belong. You've caused me nothing but trouble today!" I said.

The small masked animal turned toward me briefly before tossing its ringed tail into the air and fleeing into the neighboring garden. Wishing life were as easy for humans, I returned to the cleanup.

Three hours later, I was amazed to see that most of the work was done. My two kind helpers were like the leprechauns who came at night to finish all the shoemaker's work. "I can never repay you for your kindness." I told Wynnie and Jill.

"We were glad to help," said Jill.

"And happy to make a new friend," added her sister.

"We have to go home now. Mother needs us to set the table and help with dinner. You're welcome to join us if you like," said Jilly.

"Thank you, but Mother would tan my hide if I did such a thing," I said.

"Oh, don't your parents like the Welsh?" asked Jilly.

"No, that's not what I meant, not at all. My father says it doesn't matter whether we're German, Welsh, English, or Irish. We should all support one another.

"Then why not join us?" asked Wynnie.

"My mother would think it was ill-mannered to even consider going to your mother's table without advance warning, but thank you for the invitation."

After the girls left, I placed the laundry in the clothes press with some sprigs of fragrant lavender, picked up my few belongings, and started home. It felt like ages since I started the wearisome day. School days seemed heavenly by comparison. If Sarah and Maymie complained about doing schoolwork, I would give them a piece of my mind. Ah, for the days of sitting on the porch swing doing homework assignments...

❖ ❖ ❖ ❖ ❖

That night, after supper, Gram and Aunt Aggie came over to sit on the front porch and socialize. Gram asked me about my experience with the "dirty divils" that were running through the village that day. Evidently the dogs created havoc in several locations before I broke up the melee in Breslin's yard. I sighed after relating the day's events, saying, "And everything was so perfect until those dratted mongrels attacked my clean wash lines."

"Mol an lá um thráthnóna," said Aunt Aggie.

"Oh Aunt Aggie, you know we can't understand Irish."

"She's quoting an old adage that means, 'Don't praise the day until evening,'" said Gram. "Here in Pennsylvania the farmers say, 'Don't count your chickens before they hatch.' The meaning is the same in either language. You never know what the future holds, so don't be too optimistic," Gram warned.

"I'd rather look on the bright side than be a prophet of gloom," I said.

"Things are dismal right now," said Grammam. "It's a turrible time here in Amerikay what with this bloody Civil War going on."

"Indeed," said Aunt Aggie who was wholeheartedly against the war. "Our men are being forced into the Army because they're too poor to pay $300. 'Tis as bad as the days when the English press gangs kidnapped our boys to serve in their blasted Navy!"

"Asking American citizens to fight against the Rebs is reasonable, but it isn't fair to expect men who aren't even citizens to fight. It's a matter of justice," said Mother.

"Indeed. After all, when it comes to the better jobs in the mine, citizens are given an advantage. The Irish-born are usually shut out," Aunt Aggie said.

"Breslin said that the governor may start the draft in Pennsylvania any day now," I said.

"President Lincoln wanted all the states to begin filling the ranks weeks ago, but when the Rebs invaded Frederick, Maryland, Governor Curtin had all he could do to control things in Harrisburg," Mother said.

"Yes, Frederick is too close for comfort," said Aunt Aggie.

"Mother, will the troubles touch us here?" asked Maymie in a quavering voice.

"See, now we've scared the young ones with our talk," said Gram.

"Don't worry, Maymie. Maryland is many miles away, and the Union generals will keep the Rebs busy," I said.

"Girls, it's bedtime. Wash up and say your prayers," said Mother.

"Katie, don't forget to brush your hair one hundred strokes and rebraid it neatly. You can't go over street tomorrow with your hair lookin' like a bird's nest, or you'll be the talk of th' town," said Grammam.

"Yes, don't give those Brennans a chance to gossip." Aunt Aggie had a standing feud with Maude and Eleanor Brennan, her neighbors across the lane.

I held my tongue - for once. The day had been traumatic enough without adding an argument with my feisty relatives.

I decided I would stop by the Evans's house and thank the girls again. Tuesday was the easiest work day since baking was my finest housekeeping skill. The girls would be finished their chores by my afternoon break. I'd wrap a plate of muffins as a gift.

Making new friends was the silver lining on an emotionally cloudy day. As a result, I anticipated morning instead of dreading it. Thank goodness, my natural optimism was still intact.

CHAPTER 5

Companions

"Oh Jill, it looks like a spider's web after a windstorm," I sighed ruefully as I held up a mat of strings, my pitiful attempt at making a tatted collar.

"Don't worry, when we began tatting, mother unraveled our lacework every night. By the time my first piece was finished it was gray instead of white," laughed Wynnie.

Jill, a skilled seamstress and natural teacher, picked up the piece and plucked apart the wayward strands. She leaned over from her perch on the porch banister and showed me how to correct my errors. Today was my third lesson in making the delicate lace so valued for finery.

Every Tuesday since meeting the girls I pulled out my workbox and went over to the Evans house while waiting for the bread dough to rise. Other afternoons I took my break on Breslin's porch with the sisters. Wynnie was a fun-loving girl with a wicked sense of humor. Jill was more sedate, but she was very intelligent and had hopes of becoming a school teacher.

"Would you like to take a break and see some of the pieces we've completed?" asked Jill. I tossed down the annoying lace and leapt to my feet.

The girls led me up the narrow curving stairs to the garret and showed me embroidered tea towels, lace-edged lawn nightgowns, cutwork table linens, and other household treasures that were part of their dowries.

I held up a delicate lace collar. "How long did this take?"

"That's Jill's own design, and it only took her a week," said Wynnie with a mixture of pride and disgust.

Jill had accumulated many handwork pieces for her "hope chest" even though she did not have a suitor yet. Wynnie was three years younger so she had fewer pieces, and they were not as perfectly worked.

"Whoever I marry better hire a full household staff," Wynnie laughed as she held up a slightly misshapen towel. A wry look in my direction reminded me of the secret plan for the future that Wynnie had shared with me last week.

Jill had been at the store picking up an order for her mother last Thursday, so Wynnie and I had been alone on the porch. "Do you ever wonder who you'll marry?" was the question that led to our discussion of the future.

"Not really." I blushed, remembering the day I got my job with Mr. Breslin.

"Come on, 'fess up," demanded Wynnie. My rosy cheeks had sparked Wynnie's curiosity, and she cajoled me into telling the story.

"Thank goodness it turned out the way it did, or we may never have met."

"Yes, and now that I'm earning a good income, marriage is no longer a worry. I don't think I'd make a very obedient wife, but then again, all of the women in my family have minds of their own. I guess it all depends on the man you marry."

"What about you, Wynnie?"

"Well, I'll have to marry a broad-minded man because I plan to have a career. If you promise not to tell anyone, I'll let you in on my secret."

"My lips are sealed." I leaned toward her. All the windows were opened and sound carried.

"I want to become a pianist and create new dance hall music, like the melodies I heard in Atlantic City."

My eyes widened. "Miss Rhianwyn Evans, what will your parents say? I mean, that's wonderful, but... "

"They won't approve. My mother thinks girls should teach or do volunteer work until they find suitable partners to marry. They don't accept modern ways. I'll have to convince them."

Even though I only knew Wynnie a short time, I could see that she was more interested in creating impromptu songs than in honing the ladylike skills that most girls cultivated.

Ironically it was her family's trip to Absecon Island that led to their Wynnie's career idea. Atlantic City was a popular destination for comfortably set families like the Evanses. A few years ago, the beach was meant for invalids who looked to the bracing sea air to cure their ailments. Nowadays families visited for two week vacations, packing steamer trunks with necessities and returning home with souvenirs, shells, candy, and new sheet music purchased from vendors on the dunes. Wynnie's plan to become an entertainer was sparked by the tunes of minstrels on the beach and in the ballrooms.

After we finished discussing Wynnie's secret, I told my new friend about my family, especially about my two sisters who had hopes and dreams for the future, too.

"Sarah is very clever at Latin and literature. Sometimes her perfection is annoying, but her storytelling ability makes up for being a botheration. Even though she was only a tot when my grandfather told his stories, she inherited his ability to stir the blood of an audience."

"What about your little sister?"

"Maymie is still young, but she's very logical and she excels in history and other school subjects. I worry that both my sisters will eventually have to leave school."

"Do you miss going?"

"Yes, even though I am happy in my position, I truly

wanted to earn my diploma and get ahead in the world. My school friends and teachers already seem like a part of the distant past," I sighed.

"Some of the upper grade girls will be leaving school to get married. That's what's happening at my school. Other girls are moving away with their families for better job opportunities."

"Yes. I just heard that the O'Donnells are moving to Philadelphia. I'll really miss my good friend, Annie. I'm glad that her cousins, the Gallaghers, are not moving with them."

"What are the Gallaghers up to these days?" asked Wynnie.

The Evans girls enjoyed hearing about the Gallagher family. Everyone in the Patch, regardless of ethnic group, knew and respected Old Mrs. Gallagher. She was an herbalist and midwife that many residents of the Patch called upon in time of need since most families could not afford Dr. Atherton's fees. Deirdre Gallagher, her daughter-in-law, was a quiet lady whose gentle ways inspired confidences. Many's the time I poured out my troubles to her.

Deirdre's twin sons, Con and Dinny, were rascals who enjoyed everything the Patch had to offer. Our families were close friends, and I had known the boys since babyhood. Gram always said the boys were born with a double dose of original sin which accounted for their impish natures.

Jill and Wynnie had the opportunity to meet Con one afternoon when he passed Breslin's porch while the Evans girls and I were winding some fine linen thread. I introduced him to my friends and noticed that the Evans girls were sitting up straighter and that their eyes sparkled at his attention.

I suddenly saw Con in a new light. He was a nice-looking young man. His black hair offset his pale complexion and thick-lashed ocean blue eyes. I'd never noticed the striking combination before.

Con lounged on the steps and told us some stories that we wouldn't have heard otherwise. Boys in town who were too young to rub elbows with their elders in the saloons, had fun pulling pranks on the townspeople. One favorite pastime was to tie a cow onto a gatepost in the alley so that people coming home with a wee bit too many nips of the bottle would stumble into the creatures in the pitch dark.

"Did you hear about the Sweeney's pig last St. Patrick's Day? Con asked. "Someone dyed the poor beggar a bright green with a concoction of elder leaves and alum. None of the other pigs would go near the green squealer. It wore off eventually, but P.D. Sweeney had to divide his pigpen for a time." We all laughed at the ridiculous idea.

The worst trick was pulled by the O'Brien brothers who were the rowdiest scamps in the Patch. They put a skunk in the banker's outhouse. Luckily it was a nighttime visit to the outhouse when Mr. Rottermel confronted the critter. Since he was wearing his night shirt, at least he didn't ruin his business suit.

"Sounds like being a boy is more exciting than being a girl," said Wynnie.

"Believe me, Dinny and Con have more exciting lives than most!" I replied. "How is Dinny, by the way?" I asked.

"He's fine. Right now he's staying at the mine working an extra shift in my place," said Con. "The foreman doesn't know how to tell us apart when we plan it right. Since he's a lefty and I'm right-handed, we just have to remember which hand to use."

"Being a mirror twin is really useful for pulling pranks. When we were in third grade, Sister Rosita couldn't figure out which was which, and they'd switch seats often," I recalled.

"I'd like to meet your brother. It's hard to believe there's another young man as handsome as you are," teased Wynnie.

"Next time you're in the east end, bring Dinny for a visit," I said. "I promise scones and tea if you come after the dinner hour."

"Sure with scones as a lure, I'll bring yeh anyone you want!"

CHAPTER 6

Katie's Concerns

"Hello, Katie. What are you doing after work today?"
Wynnie came up the steps to chat as I swept Breslin's porch.
"Nothing really. I'm ahead of my chores at home since the
weather has been cooperating."

"Would you like to come over to our house around seven?
We can play checkers or look at the new Godey's magazine that
Jill got from Mrs. Jones. Some of the women at church think
ladies' magazines are too worldly, but I don't think so. Do you?"

"No, I like seeing what they're wearing in New York and
Europe and dreaming of faraway places. Thank you for the
invitation. I'll be over as soon as we clear the supper dishes."

The days flew by as I fell into a pleasant routine. Each day
was busy, but it was welcome busyness, and paid activity at
that. The Evans girls enjoyed meeting my friends, and close
relationships were building among the group of us.

Our favorite activity was spur of the moment "concerts."
Wynnie was trained as a pianist, and the twins were self-taught
musicians. Dinny played the tin whistle while Con was an expert
fiddler. Both boys were also very talented dancers. Their heavy
boots didn't hinder their energetic tapping of heels and toes on
the wooden porch. Indeed, the thumping boots added to the

beat of the jig. The Evans girls smiled and clapped. Everyone was attracted to the twins' sheer exuberance.

On warm summer evenings when he was not working, Con would stop over and visit with my family on the porch. Sarah and Maymie teased me, calling him my "beau." I glared a stern warning when Con sauntered into earshot, but my sisters just giggled and clapped both hands over their smiles. They enjoyed his visits just as much as I did.

Con even had a way cajoling the "oul wans" into smiling. When he saw Gram and Aunt Aggie walking toward our porch, Con began to sing "Treasure of My Heart." Aggie said, "Get away with yeh, yeh young spalpeen."

Con's smile crinkled his eyes and he continued to tease, imitating their Irish manner of speech, saying "Ah, Miss Aggie, don't the men in this area have eyes in their heads? Don't they have the sense they were born with? Sure they're missin' out on a fine figure of a woman, dontcha know. It's surprised I am that yeh don't have a line of suitors from here to Philadelphia."

"The back of my hand and the sole of my foot to yeh, Cornelius Gallagher," said Aunt Aggie.

"I'm amazed yer grandmother hasn't boxed yer ears, at all, at all," said Gram. But both women's eyes twinkled when he bantered with them.

One evening Con and I were sent to drive off a yowling stray cat from the hedge near the back door. Con put an arm around my shoulders when we were alone in the dark yard. It felt wonderful, but it was also alarming because my heart lurched and seemed to stop for a second. He dropped his arm as my sisters' footsteps approached.

Even before that night, I had been starting to see Con as more than a friend to race against or to debate, but it still felt awkward. Our relationship might become more than friendship, but I had mixed feelings about marriage and romance. I had a lot of plans for the future, and I still had my family to worry about, without adding a husband.

❖ ❖ ❖ ❖ ❖

I freshened my good dress with a clothes brush and fluffed up the flounced hem. My sisters and I were invited to the farewell ceili for the O'Donnell family. Annie, Rose, Molly, and their brothers, Johnnie and Daniel, were leaving for Philadelphia with their parents on the Saturday afternoon train. It was a happy event for the O'Donnells, but I was heavyhearted about my friend's departure. I would miss Annie, my partner in mischief, even though I no longer saw her every day in school. The Gallagher, O'Donnell, and McCafferty families had been close for generations, and I was unable to remember a time when we children were not friends.

Our family arrived at Boyle's barn, the site of the party, early in the evening. Annie bounded through the wide stable doors and grabbed my arm to tow me inside. Lanterns and colored paper hung from the rafters, and hay bales were neatly stacked for seating.

Annie giggled and pointed out her cousins from Ashland. She whispered, "Cousin Michael, the tall dark one, is eager to meet you after hearing of your adventures." Michael looked a bit like the twins.

P. D. Fisher and the fiddlers he had recruited were tuning up. A dance caller from Frenchtown would lead the guests in reels and jigs. My feet were already tapping. I hoped Michael and some other boys asked me to dance, but if not, I'd take to the floor with Annie or Sarah.

My insides fluttered with mixed emotions. Parties were always exciting, but this one also had an element of sadness. The reckless feeling that invaded my senses was probably what soldiers felt the night before battle. Life itself seemed to be bubbling to the surface of my skin.

The chattering voices, clacking heels, flickering candlelight, and scent of fresh hay seemed extra vibrant tonight.

The barn was getting crowded, and the noise of conversation was overwhelming. Only a few couples took to the floor at first, but as the evening advanced more dancers joined in. Overheated hoofers fanned themselves as they meandered to the cooler area outside the barn where smokers and drinkers had gathered. A few young couples wandered even farther afield to steal a few moments alone.

Con and Dinny arrived after working their shift at the mine. The twins' heads were still damp from washing up, and both boys had gleeful expressions on their faces.

"Why are the prettiest girls of Murphy's Patch outside while the fiddlers are playing?" asked Con with a wink.

"Did you wear out all your partners already?" asked Dinny.

"We were waiting for the Gallaghers to arrive for the party to begin," teased Annie.

"Let's not dillydally then!" Con grabbed my wrist and pulled me into the barn and onto the dance floor.

Dinny and Annie joined us in the reel, and I danced until my head was spinning.

When we stopped to catch our breath, the Ashland cousins came over, and Michael angled close to me. Before he was able to claim a dance, Dinny barked a warning, "We'll have none of this, Michael O'Donnell. Find your own partners. You'll not be stealing ours!"

Con's eyes cut to mine, and he winked. "I guess I should have told you more about our Katie's temper than about her charms."

Michael grinned and said, "You understated her charms, cousin." Turning to me he said, You'd not be wasting your whole evening with this rogue, would you Miss McCafferty?"

"Certainly not! But call me Katie, not Miss McCafferty. I'm practically a member of the clan, after all."

"Katie, may I have the pleasure of the next dance?" asked Michael.

"You may," I said and slanted a wicked glance at Con as I took Michael's outstretched hand.

Con did not wait long before finding a new partner, but his eyes met mine whenever I glanced his way.

The fiddlers took a refreshment break after that tune so we walked out to the barnyard. Many of the younger people were seated around a fire. Con twined my fingers between his callused ones and pulled me aside. "So flirting with my cousin Michael was to your liking, was it?"

I could not hold back a smug look at his hint of jealousy. "What girl wouldn't enjoy the attention of such a fine looking lad?" I matched his question with my own.

Though the words were teasing, a serious note lurked beneath the joking tone.

One day in late August, Con stopped by as I sat with the Evans girls on afternoon break to exchange news. I hadn't seen either of the twins in several days.

"What's been happening at the mine?" I asked. "My father likes to hear news of the job and his old friends."

"Times are hard. Since the start of the war, prices have soared and the miners can't make ends meet. Men talk about striking. An occasional mine holiday is pleasant, but no one can afford to be off work too long."

"All our friends and neighbors depend on the collieries in some way," I said.

"Without paychecks, no one in the Patch will have cash to buy anything. Eventually all the merchants, tailors, shoemakers, and railway clerks will suffer losses," Jill said. Her father owned Harry's Butcher and Victualler Shop so the Evans family's income would also be affected by losses at the mines.

"Let's hope the war will end soon so things can go back to normal," I said.

❖ ❖ ❖ ❖ ❖

That night I told my father Con's news, and he shook his head, frowning.

"Many men will be out of work if the collieries close," said Father. "But if the mine laborers don't get better wages soon, more deaths and injuries will occur."

"I don't understand."

"Accidents increase when miners struggle to produce more cars per day. The Company only pays for the coal that's brought up, not for securing roofs or clearing debris. When miners have to fill more cars each day to pay their bills, they don't have time to take proper precautions."

My mind leapt to the Gallaghers' plight. They were the perfect example of shrinking income and rising prices. Con and Dinny were the main source of earnings for their family. Deirdre and Old Mrs. Gallagher gathered herbs to make liniments and home remedies, but that didn't bring in much these days. People had no way to pay them, but they'd never turn anyone away.

"I'm worried that the twins will take chances to make money. Both of them think they're immune from harm. Con, especially, takes a lot of risks."

"Ahh, that's typical for boys their age, Katie. Those Gallagher boys are full of vinegar. Maybe they'll be lucky and escape the mines someday."

Going to bed that night, I couldn't stop worrying. I finally fell into a restless sleep, but awoke in the gray light of dawn, feeling suffocated. Fragments of a horrible dream lingered in my memory. In the nightmare I was trapped in an airless cave that kept shrinking.

Wrapped in my blanket, I went to the window for some fresh air, but I couldn't shake off the fright. Rubbing the sand from my eyes, I uncurled from my huddled position and prepared for the day ahead.

As luck would have it, work was more strenuous than usual. Before leaving for his shift Breslin said, "Katie, before Ellen and Peggy arrive, I'd like you to beat the rugs and change the curtains."

My employer was planning a nice welcome for his sister and niece. It was ironic that I was decorating for my own dismissal. Despite my best efforts, our family hovered on the brink of catastrophe. My stomach churned. What would become of us?

CHAPTER 7

Katie's Courage

"Hold on, Sarah. I have some big pieces to put in."

Rivulets of sweat rolled down Sarah's cheeks as she tilted the wooden handles upward. Wiping my brow with a dusty sleeve, I dumped chunks of coal from my long apron into the splintery barrow that Sarah tilted upwards. Since the mine strike began, picking anthracite every morning was part of the daily routine for women and children of the Patch. It was dirty, backbreaking, and dangerous labor, but after the work stoppage, life had deteriorated for everyone.

Our family suffered a loss equal to our neighbors' when Mr. Breslin's sister and niece arrived last month. Without a regular source of income, we couldn't afford to pay the rent. We were evicted from the Company house and moved in with Grammam and Aunt Aggie. Sarah, Maymie, and I slept on pallets in the living room.

One night a noise coming from the kitchen woke me. I crept to the doorway and peeked in. My mother huddled at the table, sobbing into her arms. Usually so proud and strong, she wept out all her sorrows when she thought everyone was asleep.

Our forced move had brought back the despair of the famine years when my parents received notice to leave their cottage. Now they were reliving that nightmare. I didn't know how to comfort my mother so I returned to my sleeping spot and cried myself to sleep.

Losing my job brought back a feeling of guilt that had haunted me from my earliest days. My parents had always been loving and accepting, but I felt like a disappointment. I was a girl and unable to earn a decent salary. My only brother had died as a baby fifteen years ago. I heard the biddies lamenting little James's death many times. Reliving the hurts of the past was a common practice among the old folks.

James died on the ship while crossing the Atlantic, the last member of our family lost as a result of the famine. I was born in New York as soon as the family reached America - a girl child instead of a boy.

Not that I could have replaced my parents' beloved son. Nothing could soothe the pain of seeing a sturdy, apple-cheeked toddler fade into a sickly child and die. How could anyone erase the memory of seeing his small linen-shrouded body dropped into the cold, cruel Atlantic? No funeral to aid the healing process. No grave to visit. Even if I were the smartest and strongest boy in the world, I could never replace James.

For a few months this year, the family saw me as a savior. Now I was just one more mouth to feed. The only help available for needy families came from friends, family, and the Church. With the strike going on, there were more people in need of help than people capable of helping.

Sarah brought me back to our task. "Your turn, Katie," said Sarah, stopping the wheelbarrow on level ground. I grasped the worn wooden handles and directed the barrow down the slope.

"I hope Mr. Evans gets in touch with Mother today. He said there may be a position for me at Mr. Pardee's mansion in Hazleton. Pray that it works out because I don't know how long Mother can hold up against the strain of worry, what with father and all," I said.

"At least we had Aunt Aggie and Gram to take us in," said Sarah.

"And good friends like the Evanses to help us when they can," I added.

My sister and I took turns controlling the barrow as we trudged down the trail to the shanties at the bottom of the hill. Life was hard, but at least our surroundings were glorious at this time of year. The irony was that while the mines were closed, the community did not have to suffer the dust and smoke from the colliery so everything looked cleaner. The fall leaves were especially vivid this year, and in the nearby woodlands the small animals busied themselves stashing away food for the approaching winter. We McCaffertys were only a step above the wild creatures, collecting for our own needs: coal, berries, kindling, and nuts.

As we approached the house, the smell of steam and naptha soap signaled wash day. Mother looked up from the metal boiler in the yard where she washed the linens. Sarah and I waved, then wheeled across to the back lane to dump the coal onto a small pile.

As we went to the pump to clean up, Mrs. Evans rushed over with a letter from her brother who was north in Hazleton, working with the Company to settle the strike. "Here's the note you've been waitin' for, Katie! I hope it's good tidings. God love you, you deserve it!" I clutched the crisp folded sheet before gaining enough courage to open it.

> *Miss McCafferty,*
> *As Mr. Ario Pardee's business manager,*
> *it has come to my attention that you are*
> *interested in securing employment. I*
> *understand that you are currently*
> *unemployed, but have adequate experience*
> *in performing domestic chores. Personal*

*references from your parish priest attesting
to your moral character and from Mr.
Hugh Breslin, employee of the Coxton
Works who testified about your work
habits, have arrived at the office. I am
offering you a position on the housekeeping
staff of Mr. Pardee's estate in Hazleton.
We will require your services immediately
so make arrangements to take the 10 a.m.
train on Saturday. Enclosed is a cheque
covering your expenses to the station. You
will be met and brought to Pardee Square
by buggy. As condition of your employment,
you will be provided with room and board,
two uniforms, aprons, and caps. Other
needs must be provided by yourself.*

> *Respectfully,*
> *Jabez Williams*

Waving the letter as I hopped around the yard, I shouted out the good news. "I'm being hired as a servant at the Pardee estate. I'm to leave on Saturday morning!"

The women hugged me, and we all cried with joy. Sarah ran inside to tell Father, and Mrs. Evans promised to freshen a trunk with potpourri before lending it to me. Then the hustle and bustle of packing began with everyone setting out to borrow, clean, and create luggage for my trip.

Saturday arrived, sparkling with October energy. I had my portmanteau and Mrs. Evans's trunk packed with valuables donated by kith and kin. Along with my ordinary clothes, there was a new night rail from Sarah, a tortoiseshell comb from my best friend Wynnie, towels from Mother, and an apron from Jill's hope chest in the garret. Deirdre and Mrs. Gallagher came to see me off and brought a basket of their handmade herbal soaps and toiletries. I carefully tucked my well-worn Missal and a dainty lace-edged linen handkerchief from Grammam into my handcase. Aunt Aggie's gift of a warm wool shawl, knitted in the diamond and popcorn-stitch of the Aran Isles, brought a lump to my throat.

"Go on with yeh now, girl, 'tis no time for gettin' all choked up. A new job is a happy occasion. Sure, 'tis only a few miles away yeh'll be. Yer not crossing the ocean!" I straightened my spine at Aunt Aggie's typical, brusque comments.

As much as I wanted this job, in my heart I dreaded leaving my close-knit family to work with strangers in another county. I said tearful good-byes at the local whistle stop and traveled to Mauch Chunk where I transferred to the Lehigh Valley Hazleton train. The hour length trip along the white-capped Lehigh River felt like a week. We chugged up the long mountain, glowing with fall color, to the station where I was to be met by the coachman.

As I alighted from the car, I was hailed by a deep voice with bit of a Welsh lilt. "Miss Catharine? This way please."

Escorted to the buggy and greeted by Evan Thomas, the talkative driver, we headed up the road to the Pardee estate. Mr. Thomas filled me in with details of the family and what I could expect at the estate. "Just mind yer manners and do your work, and everything will be fine. There aren't many employers who take care of their own like the Pardees."

"What's the family like, Mr. Thomas?"

"Mrs. Pardee is a fine lady and her children are mannerly, if a bit spoiled. The sons of Mr. Pardee and his first wife are off serving their country. Very patriotic, they are. In fact, Mr. Pardee just outfitted his son Ario's company at his own cost."

When we pulled into the carriageway, a tall groom came up to help me alight. "Who have we here, Mr. Thomas?" asked the young man in a strong Irish accent.

"Katie, this rackety fellow is Patrick O'Brien." Evan grinned at Patrick's rueful expression. "Pat, this is Miss Katie McCafferty. Mind your manners, man."

"Now, now, you're giving the colleen the wrong impression," said Pat. "Welcome to Pardee Square, Miss Katie. Let me know if I can help you get settled in."

The Pardee estate was heavily wooded even though it was in the very center of Hazleton. The 30-room brick mansion was only two years old. Evan opened the sturdy door of the servant's entrance, and I took a deep breath as I entered with portmanteau in hand. Evan hustled me into the summer kitchen to meet the cook and housekeeper who were discussing the menu for the evening dinner.

"Well, missy, you look as though you're capable of a day's work," said Mrs. Lane, the housekeeper. "See to it that you behave yourself, and we'll get along fine. I'll show you to the servants' quarters in the attic."

After moving into a stuffy third floor bedroom, Mrs. Lane told me to freshen up and return to the kitchen to learn the routine for serving dinner.

"M'am, could you please tell me where Mass is offered tomorrow?" I asked.

"St. Gabriel's is down on the corner of Wyoming and Chapel, but all the servants are expected to go to the Presbyterian Church across Broad Street. Mr. Pardee founded the church, and he serves as an elder there. If you want to prosper, you will be on time for services and sit in the servants' pew."

Whissht, I was flabbergasted by that news. Go to a protestant church? I wondered what the other Catholic servants did. I decided to wait until after supper and ask Patrick. When everyone had finished eating, I followed him out to the tiled hallway.

"Patrick, Mrs. Lane informed me that I'd be expected to attend the Presbyterian service on Sunday. Goodness, I am so confused. What about going to Mass?"

"Father Sheridan at St. Gabriel's told me that I still have my obligation to attend Mass but that I should obey the rules of the house regarding church attendance. He said it would be a more serious sin to lose the position that supports my family. If you'd like, I will take you to see the priest so you can hear it from his own lips."

"Thank you! I need to find out where the church is anyway, so I'd be grateful if you'd show me around."

As we walked from Broad to Wyoming, Patrick pointed out the various points of interest. Hazleton was a major town with lots of shops and saloons. There were livery stables, millinery shops, a brand new firehouse, and even a fencing gymnasium. The church was a small wooden building, but a stone church was being planned.

Father Sheridan repeated exactly what Patrick had said so I was able to go to sleep with a clear conscience, one obstacle hurdled.

Mrs. Lane initially trained me to work as kitchen maid, but after a few weeks she decided that I was capable of more challenging tasks. Thank goodness in my new position I no longer had to pamper Mrs. Pardee's spoiled lapdogs. The loathsome pugs were served tidbits of the best meat on their own silver plates and ran underfoot throughout the mansion. The Mistress even held them up and kissed their pushed in faces. Ugh! I dreaded being seen with the creatures.

Patrick teased me whenever he caught me stepping out the back door to walk the two dogs. I always peered quickly in both directions before exiting to avoid meeting anyone. It was humiliating to escort the waddling pugs in their fancy harnesses down the carriageway for their daily walks. My goodness, it would be disastrous if Dinny and Con Gallagher ever saw me parading down the street following the curly-tailed dogs with their bulging eyes.

I imagined their banter. "Hey lookit, Dinny, there goes Katie with her pet piglets. I wonder if she's off for a roll in the mud?"

"No, Con, she's taking them to get their tails recurled." My face flamed envisioning the ridiculous scene and the twins' hearty laughter. If word got out, I'd never hear the end of it! Dogwalking was one chore I was happy to leave behind.

Being promoted to parlormaid meant a pay increase so I was excited to get started. On my first day in the new position, Mrs. Lane sat me down in the pantry to demonstrate a technique for making the silver gleam like sunlight on icicles. The trick was to use the water in which potatoes have been cooked to remove the tarnish. We soaked the creamer, sugar bowl, waste bowl, and teapot for an hour, and the tarnish disappeared. After washing the pieces in sudsy water, we rinsed them well and dried them to a shine using a lot of elbow grease. I refilled the containers and set off to the drawing room for my first above stairs task as parlormaid. Carrying the tray up the back stairs was a chore, but I made it unscathed. The silver tea set was quite heavy, and I was afraid of sloshing hot liquid onto the tray. I leaned down to set it carefully on the ornately carved table. I was admiring the bright sheen of the polished silver when the mistress called, "Bridget, please close the draperies."

I looked all around the room, but didn't see anyone else. Who was Bridget anyway? I wondered.

"Bridget, the sun is blinding me, close the draperies!"

Mrs. Pardee was staring directly at me so I said , "M'am, if you are speakin' to me, my name is Katie."

Without responding, she pointed demandingly to the window with her right hand while her left shaded her eyes from the glare. I yanked on the draw cord to adjust the draperies. As I left the dimmed room, she said, "Tell Mrs. Lane to come to the parlor, Bridget."

Must be something wrong with the poor woman's hearing, I thought. I'll have to speak loudly in the future.

I returned to the servants' hall and notified Mrs. Lane of the Mistress's request. After the housekeeper was out of earshot,

I asked Daisy, the kitchen maid, whether there was anything wrong with Mrs. Pardee.

"What do you mean by 'wrong'?" asked Daisy.

"I mean, is she hard of hearing, or is she daft?"

"My goodness, no, Mrs. Pardee is perfectly fine. Why do you ask?"

"Well, she kept calling someone named Bridget, but there was no one in the room except me. I thought she mistook me for someone else, but even after I told her my name, she still called me Bridget."

Daisy broke into gales of laughter which mystified me completely. She finally sputtered out an explanation which changed my confusion to annoyance. "The Mistress is like all her kind, unwilling to bother remembering a servant's name. All the parlor maids are Bridget. It keeps us in our lowly places to deny us even our given names. After all, your name, Catharine, and my real name, Margaret, are both royal names. High falutin' names are too good for the likes of us, Katie, my dear!" said Daisy.

We'll see about that, I thought. This was another idea to contemplate as I adjusted to my new environment.

Mrs. Lane bustled into the room, her long silver chatelaine swinging from her waist. All her keys, tools, and sewing supplies were attached. Since the Pardees did not employ a butler, Mrs. Lane was the dominant force among the staff. Seeing her black gown and white lace cap determinedly bobbing down the hall set even the towering footmen trembling. I knew I must maintain my dignity, and my temper, during the scolding that I knew was coming.

"Katie, Mrs. Pardee asked me to speak to you about dawdling in response to her commands. You'll have to perk up if you want to remain an upper servant."

"Mrs. Lane, Mrs. Pardee was calling "Bridget," so I didn't respond. I'm usually snappy in performing my duties, but how was I to know what Mrs. Pardee meant? Now that I know the foolish custom, I'll play along. But I prefer being called Catharine. My name is the only thing I possess."

"If you want to keep this position, you'll have to accommodate the quirks of the wealthy. Pride must be secondary."

"Yes, m'am, I can see that sometimes it'll be to my benefit to bend a little, but there are certain things I refuse to give up." Mrs. Lane raised her eyes to the pressed tin ceiling. I guess she considered me mule-headed, but without further discussion she bustled off to the pantry while I headed to the servants' hall where the well-scrubbed table was already set for supper.

Now that I was a parlor maid, my place at dinner was closer to the head of the table where Mrs. Lane reigned supreme. Being seated in order of importance was a custom the Pardees borrowed from the aristocracy. Copying foolish British traditions seemed un-American to me. Personally, I would rather stay at the lower end of the table where Daisy and James entertained everyone. For all the democracy I could see, the Pardee servants' hall could be in England or on the Marquis of Conyngham's estate in Ireland. All these rules were driving me mad!

If only my family were close enough to visit, I'd feel more relaxed. I would love to tell them about my experiences in person, but I'd skip the low points since they'd fret. I guess letter writing was better after all.

Father always says I have a giveaway face. I hope mother hasn't been able to read between the lines of my letters. By now she should have received the money I sent for the grocer's bill.

Sitting in the pool of lamplight, I finished my letter while listening to the stories told by the other servants. Pat and James were excellent storytellers. Their ability to breathe life into the characters reminded me of my sister Sarah.

At times James had us holding our sides with laughter at the doings of his uncles and cousins. His talent at mimicry and accents could earn him a role on stage. His features changed as he imitated the drawl of the Master or the fast blather of his Uncle Dan, a man who could talk his way out of any situation. Trudging up the narrow servants' stairs to my plain attic room, I realized I had gained a substitute family.

CHAPTER 8

Conflict

A few fallen leaves rustled on the path as I exited the grounds of Pardee Square. It was hard to believe that three months had flown since I arrived in Hazleton. Autumn passed in a flash while I was busy learning all the details of my position.

I drew my shawl closer around my neck. A wintry wind cut through to the bone. My errand to the Wyoming Street tobacconist was unusual. James, the footman, was ordinarily the errand runner, but today was a special circumstance. Late this afternoon, the Pardees and their guests were due to arrive for a hunting trip prior to the holidays.

The entire staff was on high alert: polishing, cooking, scrubbing, and making up bedrooms. Dust covers were thrown off furniture that had been unused since October.

In the toasty warm kitchen, Mrs. Clarke and Daisy diced apples, ground nuts, and mashed pumpkin filling for pies and fancy tortes. I savored the luscious scent of cinnamon, ginger, and nutmeg, wishing my family could share the heavenly aroma. Even one of the succulent treats being prepared would be beyond wonderful to share with the clan at Murphy's Patch.

I was in the parlor laying wood in the fireplace and adding

pine scent to the potpourri when Mrs. Lane bellowed, "Katie, finish there immediately. I have another task for you."

I scurried down the hall to the entryway to learn the important chore.

"Here is a list of tobacco products for the gentleman. We have to fill all the humidors in the dining room and parlor and stock chewing tobacco for the hunting lodge. Tell Humphrey to put the charges on the Pardee account. Be quick about it. Cook will need you to fill the trays at five."

Leaving the Square by the side gate, I turned the corner and saw the lamplighter already making his rounds. The December days were short, and there were many lamps to light. Gusts of wind playfully rattled a few brown oak leaves still clinging to the tall trees on Broad Street. The day was gray and damp with a hint of the snow that would soon arrive.

Against the leaden sky, the white steeple of the Presbyterian Church gleamed in the last weak rays of daylight. As I crossed Church Street, the wind buffeted my face and I felt my freckled cheeks blush from the cold. At this rate my nose would be cherry red by the time I reached the shop. Thank goodness I didn't see anyone I knew!

An evening excursion was a memorable event. On an ordinary night I was inside finishing my pre-dinner chores so to peer into the well-lit establishments where clothes, hats, and furnishings were on display was exciting. At McGinty's on Wyoming Street, diners sat at small tables enjoying the 40¢ oyster special. In an hour the stores would be closed, so many people were making their final purchases, and the streets were busy with strollers and shoppers.

Farther down Wyoming, a crowd of men gathered to read the notice board in the fading daylight. The collieries regularly posted day labor jobs and work notices there. A few women mingled amongst the usually all male crowd.

My curiosity was aroused so I moved closer. My ears perked up as I heard the anger in the voices and saw scowls on the faces of the men. Some of the women looked anxious while others expressed the same outrage as their menfolk. What was causing all the commotion? When I got nearer, I saw a large official-looking notice tacked up.

Notice of Drafting

By order of Edwin M. Stanton, Secretary of War of the United States, the Service Draft begins December 6. All able-bodied men employed at Phoenix, Cranberry, Silverbrook, or Pardee holdings must report for enlistment interviews before December 12. Only those providing a substitute or paying the $300 draft commutation fee will be exempt. The quotas of certain townships of the County of Luzerne for the nine months service not having been filled, a draft will take place to fill such deficiency at the court house, in the city of Wilkes-Barre.

"Now where would a working man get $300?" one man asked.

"Sure the Company only pays us in scrip that's barely worth the paper it's printed on. I haven't seen real coins or greenbacks in two years," said a man wearing a tweed cap.

"Getting a substitute is impossible, too. Nobody's going to put his life on the line for you unless he's kin, and no one calling himself a man would ask that!"

"If you get a substitute you never have to worry, but if you pay the $300 it only counts for this draft, not for any future drafts."

"My God! How can they be so unfeeling?"

A middle-aged woman muttered that the coal operators were no better than the greedy landlords in Ireland, "Only after their own good, they are."

"They only want bodies to feed the Reb guns. Our boys and men are their cannon fodder."

"Did yeh see the number of Irish casualties in the battle of Malvern Hill?" a women wrapped in a black shawl said. "Disgraceful!"

"This is not our war. It's just making our suffering worse," said one young woman. "Why, you can't even buy flour for a loaf of bread with prices the way they are. Coffee and tea are totally beyond the reach of my purse."

"There'll be trouble over this," said a gruff-voiced man.

"Indeed!"

"They haven't heard the last of this," said tweed cap.

"Them Mollies will protect us from this scourge. Big Joe McDermott said none of his men would allow a recruitment train to leave the station with even one unwilling man," said a lad with blue marks from embedded coal on his pale, pinched face.

"I heard tell the Molly Maguires have weapons enough to force the draft officials to back down," said the gruff man.

"Hush!" said the older woman, "Tis treason yer talkin' and right here in the public thoroughfare."

The crowd murmured agreement and some people began to leave. As the crowd started to break up, I pulled my knit shawl around my face and scurried off.

It was a relief to see Humphrey's big wooden Indian just ahead. When I opened the door to the shop, the sharp scent of leaf tobacco and a gust of warm air assailed me. I handed Mr. Humphrey the list and Mrs. Lane's billing instructions. Old Humphrey seemed to be a cheerful fellow, and we made small talk as he tied up the parcels. Considering the tidy profit he was making, he should be happy.

The sum he scratched into the Pardee ledger was enough to feed the McCafferty clan for a month. It was hard to believe that one man could afford to spend such an amount on a luxury. But then again, the Pardee payroll was large and I was one of the beneficiaries of their fortune, so who was I to complain?

I collected the package and headed back to Pardee Square in the dusk. The return trip was not as pleasant as my arrival. My mind was whirring with the draft news, and the lamplight made grotesque shadows. To my stretched nerves, the rattling of brittle leaves sounded like a skeleton's clacking bones.

While I didn't have any relatives in danger of being sent to war, I did have friends who'd be in jeopardy. Con and Dinny at home, and James and Patrick here in Hazleton were of age to be drafted. The Gallagher boys were native-born Americans while Pat and James were immigrants, but that did not seem to matter to the local authorities.

People said the coal barons wanted to impress the politicians in order to keep their power and standing. The company owners didn't bother to make a distinction between immigrants and citizens when filling out the rolls.

How will people respond to the perceived injustice of the draft? To me, that was a big worry. In some places riots were breaking out, fires were being set, and workers were calling stoppages. Newspapers supporting the Union have been calling us "Copperheads." Northerners against the war were compared to those ugly vipers.

Goosebumps rose on my arms thinking about the trouble that I felt in my bones. Grammam was the one in the family with the fairy's gift. She "saw" things that hadn't happened yet. Right now I could almost see misery looming over the region like a poisonous cloud and threatening me personally. Maybe I had inherited Gram's "gift." It seemed more like a curse.

"Whissht!" Fear caused me to shudder more than the cold damp air. A sigh of relief escaped my throat as the tall wrought iron gate leading to Broad Street clanged behind me.

I had barely stepped over the door sill of the mansion when Mrs. Lane's commanding voice hit my eardrums. "Catharine, fill the humidors with cigars and put the tobacco for pipes in the leather pouches in the library. The men will be gathering there after dinner."

One thing about work is that it takes your mind off your worries - at least for a time. I pushed the upsetting news and Sarah premonitions to the back of my mind.

When I finished in the library, I hurried to the kitchen to help Mrs. Clarke and Daisy. I reached the table just as the clattering hooves and creaking wheels heralded the arrival of the master and his guests. My evening sped up from that point onward.

The visitors were shown to their perfectly appointed rooms to freshen up, then escorted to the formal dining room. Extra servants had been hired for the visit so James, Daisy, and I not only needed to do our own jobs, but we also had to direct the temporary servants.

Huge tureens of thick hot chowder, and heavy platters of quail, beef, venison, and hare were brought up the back stairs. The side dishes were cook's specialties: preserved tomatoes, roasted potatoes, corn relish, and glazed carrots. Spicy and savory aromas mixed with the pleasant scent of melting beeswax from the glowing tapers on the table. The sideboard groaned with silver bowls, desserts, cheese trays, and a huge centerpiece loaded with fall fruits and flowers.

As I stood at attention beside the buffet waiting for the mistress's signal to remove courses, I couldn't help but overhear the conversation taking place among the guests.

Mrs. Pardee entertained the ladies with an amusing story, while another group compared the stage shows in Philadelphia and New York.

The most interesting gossip however, was Mr. Pardee and Mr. Coxe discussing the war. Mr. P. was highly involved since his eldest son was Union captain. Both men were powerful landowners who benefitted from the increased demand for coal during the war. Both wanted a Union victory.

"Ario, what do you hear from the Pardee Rifles?" asked Coxe.

"My son tells me that the shock of the Confederate advance has shaken Union troops. It's a crucial point in the war."

"Copperhead resistance here in Luzerne County is growing. Organized groups like the Knights of the Golden Circle and the Molly Maguires are recruiting in the area. The miners are against the war, and especially against the draft. News of heavy bloodshed has reached their ears."

"I submitted a list of all my employees to the draft commissioner. The ungrateful Irish are especially unwilling to repay America for their good fortune."

"I told Curtin we need troops to come and settle matters on the day of the draft registration until the train departs. I hear tell the rioters can outfit 3000 men with weapons. The government better be equally prepared."

"If these miners want a fight, they'll find they have one on their hands. The troops will report ..."

Just then I spotted Mrs. Pardee waving away the course. Judging from the annoyed look on her face, she must have been motioning to me for a few moments. Drat, bad timing! I hustled over to the dining table and removed the empty plates and leftovers.

Jenny and Molly helped remove the dishes, and within ten minutes the guests' forks flashed as they tucked into the beautiful pies and tortes. The staff relaxed for a few minutes and anticipated the leftover delicacies. We felt euphoria over our successful job so conversation was brisk as we cleared the coffee cups and dessert dishes. Soon we'd be savoring our own supper.

After eating, we relaxed near the kitchen fire and rested our weary muscles. As parlor maid, I had one last task, to straighten the library. The gentlemen had gone there after dinner to smoke cigars and drink expensive cognac while debating business issues and national events.

I tiptoed up the stairs to avoid disturbing the household and had my hand on the crystal doorknob before realizing that the men were still conversing inside. Once again, I found myself eavesdropping on information being bandied between high-powered men.

"Morgan, Ario was telling me at dinner that there's a plan to shoot any man who attempts mischief at draft registration. We need to be tough against these cowards and troublemakers," said Coxe.

"I agree, the labor force can't be allowed to dictate to industry. These men need to respect their betters and be taught a lesson," a deeper voice added. "That fellow, Joe McDermott from Shenandoah, is the ringleader. He and his gang are looking for retribution."

"There are recruiters for the Knights of the Golden Circle in the area, too. They meet in clusters called "castles" and have made inroads with the German farmers and even Americans of good nativist stock."

"I've heard McDermott's gang called Buckshots and Molly Maguires," said Mr. Pardee.

"If men from my collieries make trouble, they'll learn what happens to traitors to the Union, which is what these trouble-makers are," said Heckscher, who spoke with a strong New York accent. "I have a blacklist of people who have been heard conspiring, and they'll never work in the coal region again. And if anyone is caught with specific information, his punishment is jail... or worse!"

"Here, here," agreed my employer.

"Well, Ario, gentlemen, please excuse me. I'm ready for some rest after this long day of travel. I'll see everyone early at breakfast before we leave for the shooting lodge.

Murmuring and movement indicated that the group was breaking up and going to their bedrooms for the night. I scurried behind the heavy velvet portières at the end of the hallway to avoid being noticed. Luckily, all five men went in the opposite direction toward the stairs so I was undetected.

After I was certain that no one remained on the first floor, I went into the library to air and straighten the room. I took all the used crystal and ashtrays to the kitchen where Tweeny waited to wash them.

"What took you so long?" she asked.

"I couldn't interrupt the gentleman by entering," was my evasive response. I escaped to my attic room to compose my thoughts and decide what to do with the unexpected information.

At my break the next day I composed a letter to Con. I needed to know what was happening in the Patch. I hoped that Con and Dinny and my friends from St. Anne's were not involved in anything that would get them into trouble with the authorities.

CHAPTER 9

Christmas at Pardee Square

"A tree? In the house?" Pat and James laughed when I shook my head at the doings in the parlor. Mrs. Pardee had ordered the strongest servants to remove some heavy pieces of furniture to make room for a ten foot tree.

"The ways of the wealthy are strange, Katie. When you have too much money it scrambles your brain," said James.

"Guess my senses will never be addled then," I said.

"Mrs. Pardee imported all the decorations and candle-holders from Germany. Christmas trees are a popular tradition there," said Pat.

"Here, here, get to work and stop gossiping about your betters," said Mrs. Lane, who had only heard Pat's last comment.

Mrs. Lane directed the staff in decorating the branches with candles, glass balls, and tin ornaments. James's towering height and long arms were needed to reach the highest branches. The candles sat on the boughs in cleverly designed pendulum holders that were balanced by weighted stars. With the candles lit, the dangling glass balls and tin ornaments reflected a soft radiance. Baby Frank reached out a chubby hand to grasp the colorful objects, but his nursery maid whisked him out of range.

Once the evergreen was in place, I had to admit the piney

aroma and cheerful appearance was a welcome change from the parlor's usual stuffy atmosphere. A Christmas tree was a lot of work, but the finished product was lovely. As I stepped back to admire the effect, small fists tugged on my uniform skirt.

"Katie, Katie, look how I stayed in the lines!" Six-year-old Bart Pardee and his older brother, Izzie, were helping to decorate, cutting out Thomas Nast's newspaper sketches of Santa Claus and coloring them. I complimented the boys and cut pieces of tinsel garland to tie their artwork onto the tree.

My favorite display was the three-tiered pyramid contraption on a side table. The draft created by small red candles moved wooden paddle blades, and a carved Nativity scene twirled before my fascinated eyes. I wished my sisters could see the delights. At least I was able to take the stubs when the candles were replaced. I would send them to Murphy's Patch so a candle would remain burning in our window through the Christmas season.

Attending to the constant stream of guests kept me too busy to leave the grounds. I kept my ears perked for news from the outside world whenever I served refreshments in the main rooms. Businessmen who visited the mansion discussed the war effort with Mr. Pardee. Some were worried about an assault on the coalfields by Confederate troops.

The newspaper was my main source of information. When I delivered the freshly ironed sheets to the study every day, I always scanned the pages for news from Big Mine Hill or Tamaqua. Articles about labor troubles, the war effort, and the local response to the draft were published daily.

I eagerly awaited letters from home. My sisters' short notes did not tell me anything beyond household news and school gossip, but Con's response to my letter confirmed my fears about the effect of the war on the Patch. While men continued to volunteer, some resented the Company's handling of enrollment lists. Families losing their breadwinners were beginning to commend the resistance groups.

Con's attitude alarmed me. He and Dinny were now old enough to spend time in the taverns and join the Ancient Order of Hibernians, and his letter showed that he had picked up a more cynical attitude from the older men. He was very negative about the upcoming draft, and scoffed at Mr. Pardee's threat to blacklist draft resisters. He boasted that, if necessary, they would block the draft train from leaving the Pottsville depot.

Knowing my friends' attraction to deviltry made me more concerned than ever. Con also laughed off my questions about secret societies, saying that the Company men were listening to Benjamin Bannan's nonsense and making a mountain out of a molehill.

Con's letter only increased my thirst for news.

Was it really only months before that I had happily pored over fashion magazines with Wynnie? Times had surely changed. The news sections of the newspaper captured all my attention. Mrs. Pardee, however, devoured the social page and advertisement section. One afternoon she announced a shopping trip to the Kristkindlmarkt in Pottsville. The outside fair would feature imported gift items for Christmas. German cuckoo clocks, Moravian stars, creche scenes, and intricate toys for the younger children were among the items for sale.

Mrs. P. planned to buy a large ceramic stein for her stepson, Ario, Jr. Mr. Pardee hoped that his sons would be in Hazleton for the family Christmas celebration. If not, their gifts would be sent to them at Union encampments where "the boys" were stationed. Mrs. Pardee started planning a trip by train to the city. The most exciting news was that I would attend Mrs. Pardee and the children.

Though I was pleased to see the city, my greater concern was that I would have a chance to intervene in the situation that Con and his friends had started. On the day of departure, we hustled to the station with enough luggage for several days. Porters carried the bags onto the train, but I would be in charge of everything once we were on board. A reddish-brown car with crisp gold lettering was already pulled up at the siding. I was more excited than Izzie and Bart since we were traveling in a luxury box with soft leather seats and plush velvet hangings for privacy. Our tickets gave us access to the lounge car and other exclusive areas that I had never seen before. To give Mrs. Pardee some quiet time, I took the two children for a walk through the cars to the observation deck.

"Oh, look at the horses in the field... and the hex sign on that barn." I pointed out the green-glazed windows at highlights of the landscape to keep the children occupied. When we went back to our berth, we played counting and memory games until the children were lulled into naps. The lurching of the train stopping at Pottsville station awoke the children, and we gathered our possessions and left the car.

A coachman was waiting for us at the brick P&R station when we alit from the train amidst a cloud of steam, and he swept us by carriage to Pennsylvania Hall where a luxury suite was set aside for the Pardees. Visiting coal barons to the Schuylkill County seat always stayed in the hotel's deluxe accommodations. Even my room, on the least exclusive floor, was delightful. I bounced onto the wide bed and giggled as I was almost launched off the other side.

I freshened up and had a cold luncheon before going to the outdoor market with Mrs. Pardee and her sons. The street scene was bustling with excitement. Large kegs at the intersections blocked out traffic to provide safe travel for pedestrians through small wooden booths and canvas-covered displays.

Mrs. Pardee examined and ordered many items. Some were

to be personalized or created especially to her taste. The children wove between people in the crowd and raced each other from booth to booth.

"Boys, stop!" I chased them down a crowded lane and scolded them. "Your mother is looking for you."

"Mother, can I buy something?" asked Bart, pointing at a toy display.

"Nothing for yourself, but you may purchase something for your brothers and sister." Mrs. Pardee took note of their choices for Christmas gifts. The long day was beginning to wear on the boys, and they started to push each other and bicker.

"Time to return to the hotel," said Mrs. Pardee amidst complaints from her sons.

Once Izzie and Bart were settled with a maid from the hotel to oversee their supper, Mrs. Pardee and I returned to the market to choose items for the children. By five o'clock the vendors had fires and lamps lit to allow their customers to see their merchandise. The festive scene was very enjoyable and since I was wearing my warmest outer garments, including gloves and scarf, the bite of the cold air did not affect my pleasure. Every breath filled my lungs with the smell of chestnuts, pretzels or spicy sausages roasting on open grates. Candles, incense, toasted candied peanuts, gingerbread, and other exotic scents mingled in the air. Laughter and music met my ears. It was as much a social event as it was a market.

My employer smiled and discussed the merchandise with the vendors, but her good mood disappeared when time came to order. Spoiled by the constant pandering of merchants in Hazleton and Philadelphia, Mrs. Pardee was dumbstruck that she would have to wait for some of the items.

Turning to me with a stern look she said, "You'll have to stay in the city two extra days to collect my purchases and ensure their quality."

"Yes, M'am." I answered in a demure way, but beneath my

composed face I was delighted. Here was my chance! The opportunity I had been hoping for had fallen into my lap. I would gather my courage and conduct some very serious business.

Annoyed that she would have to take the trip back without my help, Mrs. P. pushed a purse into my hands and gave me last minute instructions. The money was to pay for the orders, for cab fare and tips, and for the return trip to Hazleton. She and the children bustled off to the station to catch the train home.

That evening I selected some literature in the lobby since I didn't dare go out alone. Later, in my room, I planned what I would say to Mr. Benjamin Bannan. I wanted to sound the alarm without becoming one of those most hated characters, an informer.

Early the next morning I set out on my mission. One of the bellboys was especially friendly so I approached him to ask directions to the *Miners' Journal and Pottsville Advertiser* office. I was lucky in my choice since he not only gave me directions, but also called a cab and refused the tip I offered.

"Sure you need the money more than I do, darlin'. Buy yourself something at the fair. But why a nice Irish lass would be going to the *Journal's* office is a mystery to me."

The cab lurched off before I could refuse the bellboy's generosity, but I had an idea of what I'd buy with the unexpected spending money. The leather seat sighed as I settled into it. I pondered the meaning of his parting comment as I gazed out at the passing scenery.

When I arrived at the *Journal's* office on Mahatongo Street, I paid the driver and stepped onto the slate sidewalk. I stared at the ornate gold lettering on the glass window and composed my thoughts. Taking two deep breaths, I held the air in my cheeks for a moment then puffed out a cloud of steam through pursed lips. Feeling more confident, I straightened my shoulders and grabbed the brass doorknob.

Inside, the office was bustling with activity. Men wearing green visors hovered around paper-stacked desks composing and correcting articles. Other staff members were opening mail or conferring with their colleagues. A man rushed in with a steel engraving asking if he was in time for the issue's deadline.

"Excuse me, miss, may I help you?" I turned toward a quieter area of the main room where a desk was positioned in front of a frosted glass office door. The receptionist raised his eyebrows when I gave him my name and told him I was interested in meeting with Mr. Bannan. He jotted down my name, then knocked on the door of the inner office.

I couldn't hear what Bannan's assistant said, but I heard a chair scrape across the wooden floor and a booming voice.

"Are you mad, Spencer? I don't have the time to chit chat with a ragamuffin from shantytown. That whole mob of riffraff should be sent back to the godforsaken island they came from. You know how I feel about all those hooligans. They're all cut from the same cloth, useless bunglers. Show her the door."

Spencer returned to his desk and sat across from me, straightening papers and avoiding my glance. "Miss McCafferty, Mr. Bannan is not available this afternoon and does not have time for an appointment later this week."

"Very well then, Benjamin Bannan is missing an important opportunity, but from what I just heard, he has his mind made up. I'll have to take my information elsewhere." I stood and flounced my skirts, then marched to the exit. My right hand, outstretched to grasp the brass doorknob, trembled with the effort not to slam the door. The bellboy's mystifying comment made sense now. Bannan, the editor and draft commissioner, was a bigot.

When my heart stopped pounding and my heated blood cooled, I felt deflated. What now? I'd have to work out another way of stopping the bloodshed that was sure to happen if the McDermott's men met the hired guns of the mine owners.

If at first you don't succeed, try, try again. I still had some time to develop a new strategy. Meanwhile I decided not to allow Bannan to ruin my day. Walking to the cab station on the corner, I thought about what I could buy my parents and sisters at the market. The small drawstring bag in which I kept my money clinked as I jiggled it. I wished that I had more money. It would be difficult to stretch the funds four ways.

Just as the thought entered my mind, I had a brainstorm. The ticket! I searched through my bag and located the return ticket that Mrs. Pardee pushed into my hand last night. It was a first class seat! My emotions soared. I could exchange the expensive ticket for a cheap seat in a combination car. I didn't mind traveling with the ordinary passengers and baggage, especially since it meant several extra dollars in my purse.

I sallied off to the street fair feeling like a wealthy capitalist. My first purchase was simple. I decided to purchase some fragrant spices and a cookie press shaped like an angel for my mother, the baker.

The next stall has wonderful three-tiered pyramids like the one at Pardee Square. The carving and paintwork on the tiny figures was exquisite, but the prices were far beyond my pocketbook. Fortunately a little farther along I came to a booth with small German woodcarvings. One piece, depicting a trio of girls playing Ring a-ring o'roses, reminded me of my sisters and me in early childhood. My father would appreciate both the subject and the quality of the piece, so I added that gift to my basket.

My sisters would be happy with some candy, but should it be fudge, sugar mice, parma violets, barley toy candy, or rock candy strings? Apothecary-style jars lined the open shelves in the rear of the stand with more choices than I had ever seen in one place. The colorful and tempting plate of broken candy for sampling helped with my decision. Red and green barley pops finished my shopping list.

I swung the string-wrapped parcels and imagined my family's delight on Christmas morning. I collected the merchandise for Mrs. Pardee and returned to the hotel. Passing my friend the bellboy, I smiled and told him that my little sisters would appreciate his kindness on Christmas morning.

"How did your meeting with Bannan go?"

I confessed that the appointment never materialized.

"I'm not surprised. Bannan is a member of the Know Nothing Party. He uses that paper of his to belittle us. He detests Irish Catholics. Calls us drunks and vermin."

"How did he become Draft Commissioner?" I asked.

"Benjamin Bannan curries favor with the political leaders and the coal operators. He gives them free advertising space in *The Journal.* One hand washes the other."

"Thank you for your help. I'll have to find another way to achieve my goal." Hopefully plan number two would be more successful.

CHAPTER 10

Catastrophe

New Year's Day 1862 began with prayers for the year to come, for peace to be restored. Mrs. Lane permitted the house staff to attend Mass - provided we returned promptly to serve the midday meal.

Father Sheridan, standing tall in the pulpit, addressed the problems faced by his congregation. Obey the law and report for the draft was his stern advice. He suggested ways for people who were against war to serve without engaging in combat.

I glanced around the church. Murmurs and squirming in the pews indicated the discomfort of some parishioners at the pastor's stance. Others amongst the congregation nodded in agreement with the homily.

I feared that Father Sheridan's sermon would not be heeded by everyone. The tension in the community had grown since November. Throughout the holiday season, I saw groups of men huddled near corners and notice boards, but they always dispersed when a well-dressed gent or law officer came within hearing. Their furtive looks and mutterings about "$300 men" made me wonder what was planned for the day of the draft.

During the second week of January, as I removed garlands of evergreen festooning the mansion's leaded glass doors, I saw an old neighbor from Murphy's Patch striding up Broad Street. I was so excited to see a familiar face that I hailed him from a distance. "Mr. Daley, what a surprise! Are you in Hazleton on errands? It's so good to see you!"

He met me at the gate before responding. "Katie my dear, I hate to dash your spirits, but I'm here to give you a message..."

As he said the words, I noticed his solemn face and stiff posture. He was steeling himself to impart bad news. A sharp pain tore through my center, and I clutched my throat, choking back a sob.

My voice quavered. "Is it ...Father?"

"Yes, love, your Mother wanted you to know that the chill he caught last week has worsened his condition. When he takes a deep breath, a harsh rattle echoes in his chest. I'm sorry to say the end may be near. Old Mrs. Gallagher came and tended him, but her herbal remedies didn't help your da. The doctor would've done no better though."

"Oh God, I should be at home!" Mr. Daley tried to comfort me with kind words, but I was heartsick. Maybe if I had started working sooner we would have had the medicine Father needed. The money I sent home was never sufficient! Even if I were a lady's maid I could not have made enough to support the family. Only men's jobs paid adequately, and not all of those did. My grief changed to anger. The unfair cost of being poor and female infuriated me.

I had to get home. If I could get ahead in my duties, maybe I would be granted leave. In such a situation even the strictest of masters usually showed sympathy. I spent an anxious day worrying until Mrs. Lane informed me that I would be allowed compassionate leave of three days.

Quickly packing my bag, I arranged to travel by the cheapest means possible: stagecoach. It would waste one of my available days, but I did not have the fare to go by train. Poor

Mother would be fretting, but there was no way to notify her of my arrival.

During the long trip I concentrated on sitting still. Fidgeting relieved some of the pent up energy, but my fellow passengers glared at me whenever I shifted in my seat. I stared out the window maintaining a stoic exterior, but anguish was ripping me apart. Would Father be alive to hear me say goodbye?

The landscape outside finally began to look familiar. As the stagecoach arrived in the Patch, I heard deep voices shouting orders, then the dreaded sound of the colliery's emergency whistle. The memory of my father's accident flooded my mind.

I felt a sick chill curl inside my body. I clutched my stomach and gulped several times to overcome the urge to be sick. I was certain to know the victim of today's disaster. Someone I knew would be missing a father or son, husband or brother today. And every family in the Patch hoped it would not be them.

I joined the stream of people rushing to the mine. A large crowd was already gathered, knots of men clustered together talking urgently while terror-stricken women clutched rosaries or held the hands of toddlers.

"Which shaft?" "What happened?" "A blast, did you say? How many got out?" "Who?" Everyone was shouting at once.

"Firedamp exploded, bringing down some bad cribbing," said a begrimed miner. Someone in the crowd said that several miners had been warned by escaping rats, but laborers who were deep in the shaft were caught beneath fallen beams and gob.

The foreman stepped onto a platform and the crowd went dead silent. He started calling out the names of the men still trapped inside the mine. "Sam Boyle... Dwight Lewis ... Thomas Devlin... Miles Carr... Evan Davis... and Con Gallagher.

CHAPTER 11

Consequences

"Con!" I felt my knees weaken as a gray haze passed across my eyes. Con, my dear friend. Con, the prankster. Oh God, please don't take Con. Haven't the Gallaghers suffered enough?

Deirdre Gallagher, Con's mother, stood in white-knuckled silence with the other women while rescuers feverishly hoisted debris from the opening of the shaft. Con had been exiting on a mule car when the gas exploded, so he was the first victim recovered from the mine.

As they pulled Con from the rubble, his mother's stoicism crumbled. Blood smeared his shredded clothes. Con's legs had been crushed in the blast. Deirdre saw her son's fine features drained of his usual fresh color and vibrant expression. She wailed a keening shriek and sank to the ground. She reached her arms toward her unconscious son, and the laborers carefully lowered him into her lap. She gently gathered his body across her full black skirts, draped over the dusty ground. Her shawl hung forlornly down along the sides of her stark white face as she cradled his limp form.

The men had tied ropes around each of his damaged legs and had tightened them with a stick to stop the bleeding.

Laborers held the tourniquets and tried to swab away the blood. Mrs. Gallagher smoothed the hair off her son's brow.

A transport cart barreled around the corner while volunteers rushed to get rescue equipment amid the shouts and activity outside the mine shaft, but near the tableau of mother and son, time seemed to stand still.

The strange, subdued scene was broken by a silver-haired figure who forced her way through the somber crowd with jabs from a blackthorn stick. The old woman, dressed head to toe in black, commanded respect. With blue eyes blazing, she asked, "What's happened here?"

Seeing Deirdre caring for the boy on the ground, she whipped around to face the man who was holding the list of victims. The foreman approached the startling figure, realizing that it was Old Mrs. Gallagher, the twins' grandmother.

"Who's to blame for this? Who takes responsibility?" The Gallagher matriarch's glare scorched him with fury.

"Now, Mrs. Gallagher, accidents DO happen. We all know that mining coal is a dangerous job," said the foreman, trying to calm the fierce old woman.

"Accident, my foot! Shoddy safety and greedy owners caused this devastation!"

"Our safety record is..."

"Reprehensible is what it is. You exploit your laborers. You take their strength and health, then cast them aside. This Company killed my husband and my son, and now this."

"We're lucky that the accident was not ..." The foreman faltered when he saw her unquenchable rage.

"Lucky, is it? My grandson was a good lad, but not a lucky lad. This boy was our hope for the future. This boy was IMPORTANT."

Her full-throated cry sent a shiver through the crowd. She raised her face and a clenched fist to the leaden sky. "God, deliver us from this evil!"

Turning her anger on the crowd, she shouted, "Isn't there a man among you? Won't anyone take a stand against this wickedness before more lives are lost?"

Heads dropped. A feeling of shame flooded through me. We were all in some measure to blame, sheep dumbly marching to the slaughter.

Looking directly at the foreman, Mrs. Gallagher thundered, "Don't you even know the names of your men? Are they so unimportant to you? You know the names of the mules that haul the cars, don't you? DON'T YOU? Well, that lad is our Dinny, not Con!"

Dinny! Yes, I had known that it was Dinny, but anguish hadn't allowed the realization to sink in. The twins must have exchanged places as they had on many other occasions. The foreman assumed it was Con because he was scheduled to work that day.

My God, Con would be inconsolable with grief and guilt. I scanned the crowd of villagers without seeing him. Where could he possibly be?

Old Mrs. Gallagher knelt to examine Dinny. After a meticulous inspection of his wounds, she declared that the injuries would not be fatal. When the doctor arrived, he agreed that Dinny might indeed survive the accident with proper care, but his legs could not be saved.

The horses to pull the Black Mariah finally arrived, and the men separated Deirdre from her son. She and her mother-in-law walked alongside the wagon as it lurched toward their house.

At the mine shaft, the laborers struggled to dig out the other men and boys. An air shaft was drilled once the exact location of the victims was pinpointed. Muffled cries and knocking could be heard, faintly echoing up the shaft. As painful as the sounds were to hear, silence would be worse.

Since I knew I could not help in the rescue effort, I headed to Gram's house where our family was dealing with our own troubles. My mind was reeling.

Dinny's life hung in the balance, but even if infection did not kill him, the loss of his legs would destroy his spirit. Fun-loving lad, speedy tag player, a boy who danced with wild abandon .... no longer to participate in any of those things!

Equally horrible was the thought of Con blaming himself. I have seen young men who returned from battle looking like empty husks. Would this be Con's fate?

When I reached Gram's house, I saw my sister, Maymie, on the porch looking toward the mine. Word had not reached them yet. I hugged my mother and told her the bad news. She indicated that Con was up with my father in the small bedroom. Now I knew why Con had not responded to the mine whistle. He was here, at my father's bedside. I would have to break the news about Dinny.

I hastened up the narrow stairway, churning with mixed feelings. I dreaded telling Con the news, but I was relieved that I had made it home in time to speak to my father.

When I entered the room, Con leapt from his bench. Father greeted me with a warm look. I patted my father's hand and crouched down to speak to him.

His voice was low and husky, but understandable. "Con and I have been having an important discussion which concerns you, Katie darlin'."

"Ah, Father, don't bother yourself about me at a time like this." I turned to look at Con across the narrow cot. I knew I must give Con the bad news, but I dreaded telling him. He picked up on my somber expression.

"What's wrong, Katie?"

I beckoned to Con to join me in the hallway to avoid disturbing my father.

"There was an explosion in the shaft, and I'm afraid that Dinny...."

"God, Dinny! NO! Is he ... alive?"

"Yes, but his injuries are severe, and he's lost a lot of blood."

"I must go." Con was already halfway down the hallway. I followed him downstairs. "Is Dinny still at the shaft?"

"By this time, he'll be home. Your grandmother and mother are tending to his injuries. If anyone can heal him, they can. But Con... I think Dinny has lost his legs."

"Oh, God! Does he know?"

"No, he wasn't conscious when they put him in the cart."

"I was supposed to work this morning, but I needed to see your father and ask him something before you arrived. But no time for that now. I must go!" He rushed from the house before I had a chance to offer my help.

Overwhelmed, I returned to my father and reached down to adjust his blankets. "Con had to leave. Is there anything I can get for you, Da?" I asked. "Are you comfortable?"

"I'm as well as can be expected, macushla." His voice was husky, and a reedy sound escaped his throat between words. "You know I haven't much time left. Before I leave this vale of tears, I want to thank you for supporting your mother and the girls. Take care of each other."

"I'll do my best to provide for their education. I'm going to work to improve things for people in the Patch, especially for the women."

"Catharine, you can't save the world."

"But this war and the big coal companies are hurting our people."

"Do as you always do, treat others with great love, but don't worry about great deeds. We're only in this world for a short span."

"Do you believe only men can do great deeds?"

"No, Katie, I'd give the same advice to any of my children, be they daughters or sons."

"I have to try to change things, Father. It's impossible to keep quiet seeing all the injustice."

"Let your conscience be your guide." Father was always willing to let us carve out own paths. "But enough about the world's problems. What of yourself, Catharine? If you plan to wed, you could do worse than marry into the Gallagher clan. I've given my blessing to a match between you and Con, if that's what you decide."

"Con wants to marry me? To be honest, I've never considered that possibility."

At one time I may have considered a proposal, but in the last few months so much had changed.

"Are you worried I'll be an old maid, Da?" I teased.

"I'd be proud of you, Katie, whatever you'd decide. You've been a brave lass to move away and work to keep the household running, but remember ... you mustn't sacrifice your entire life."

"I'm happy earning a living. I just wish I made more money. I'm sorry I couldn't provide more for your comfort."

"You've done more than enough, Kate! Your strength and optimism have kept us going. I thank God that He gave you to us fourteen years ago, a fine healthy baby to bring your mother back to life after the tragic trip from Ireland."

My heart filled as I absorbed his words. Tears flooded my eyes, but I dashed them away. Our time together was too precious for weeping.

Father spoke for another hour before falling into a deep sleep. He had never regretted the lack of a son. Sitting next to the bed, I felt as if a flower bloomed inside me, healing my self-inflicted wounds. I slept more soundly that night than I had since autumn.

In the morning, Sarah brought Father tea, soda bread, and stewed fruit, but nothing tempted him. He had difficulty sipping the tea, and his cough had worsened. He spent the day alternately dozing, then stirring to gasp weakly.

I stayed with Father through the early hours and rose when I heard Wynnie's voice at the door. I rose quickly and hugged my dear friend.

"Katie, I'm so glad you're home. How is your father?"

"Not good. He's in God's hands now. Today he's much quieter."

"I just came from the Gallaghers' house. Dinny is under a heavy dose of laudanum, but he moans and tosses in his sleep."

"How do you find the rest of the family?"

"Con and Mrs. Gallagher are raging, and their fury is fueling them. Deirdre is stony silent, sitting in the corner, rocking and praying. The good news is that the wound is clean and even now shows signs of healing."

That night while my mother was preparing him for sleep, Father began coughing harshly. His thin chest rattled with the effort. Mother held a handkerchief to his mouth, and bright red blood stained the linen.

"Maymie, Sarah, come here!" Mother's tone of voice held a note that brought the entire household running. We gathered around the bed, and I knew the end had come. Father's angular profile had sharpened with loss of weight, and the vibrant flame within his auburn hair was extinguished.

"Look, Mary. It's James..." Father gestured weakly to an empty corner of the room. We turned to look, but saw nothing. When we glanced back at Father, we realized he had taken his last breath. A peaceful look had replaced the suffering on his face. Each of us knelt beside the bed, clutched one another, and wept, though we knew Father's torment was over at last.

CHAPTER 12

Katie's Consolation

"Ar dheis Dé go raibh a anam. 'Tis sorry I am for your troubles, Catharine," said old Mr. Clarke.

"Goodbye, sir, thank you for coming."

"Katie, let me know if there's anything we can do," said Ellen Malloy.

"I appreciate the offer, Mrs. Malloy. Thank you for coming."

Repetition made my words of appreciation feel meaningless. I'd been greeting neighbors and friends since early afternoon. Mourners still lined the room where Father's mortal remains lay. Red vigil lamps placed at both ends of the wake table flickered in the draft as the door repeatedly opened and closed. The scent of melting beeswax mixed with the camphor smell of unaired wool. Neighbors, dressed in their Sunday best, paused to view Father's body and pat the cold hand entwined with worn black rosary beads. A threadbare velvet kneeler allowed people to offer a prayer before extending condolences to our family. Mother, my sisters, and I stood near the table receiving mourners. Gram and Aunt Aggie sat in stiff, straight-backed cane chairs borrowed from Mr. Breslin. They were like weathered oak trees, buffeted by the winds of life, but still standing fast.

In the back room, a group of church women set out the

traditional baked meats. Father's old friends, who had been in the house since noon, were playing macham. A glass of whiskey and a hand of cards were laid out in front of an empty chair in father's memory.

The Gallaghers, who were dealing with their own family tragedy, took time to mourn with us. Most of the people left at midnight the night before, but several of my mother's friends stayed all night, keeping vigil.

Wakes were complex events. Tears mixed with laughter. Distant relatives who traveled into town for the funeral shared happy reminiscences from our father's childhood. Their stories emphasized his kindness, dry wit, and patience. The cousins also told us how proud he was of his trinity of daughters.

Friends, who were no better off than we were, had scrounged to donate food, tobacco, snuff, and whiskey for the mourners. A collection from father's coworkers supplemented by the Benevolent Society paid the burial costs. It was a comfort to know we were supported by the community.

The Evanses came to pay their respects early in the evening. I accompanied Wynnie and Jill to the porch when they left. I welcomed the brief respite from the cloying atmosphere inside.

The yard was just as crowded as the parlor. Old men hunkered on the porch steps smoking clay pipes. Women wrapped in shawls and their husbands wearing suits lined the path into Gram's house, murmuring greetings with people who were departing as they waited to enter. The evening was long and emotional, but we took turns keeping vigil with Father's body before falling exhausted into our beds at the end of our assigned times.

Before the coffin was nailed shut in the morning, I tucked a note in the casket, then left the room. I couldn't bear to hear the thud of the coffin lid or the hammering of the mallet. I wiped away my tears before going out to take my place in the funeral cortege.

A hundred people fell in line behind the coffin as we processed to St. Joseph's. An even longer trail of coworkers and friends went to the cemetery after the Requiem Mass. Members of the Benevolent Society donned black sleeve garters and acted as pall bearers. Con Gallagher, aged far beyond his years, served in the honor guard.

During the past two days, I had visited the Gallaghers at every opportunity. Dinny was in terrible pain and hadn't accepted the loss of his legs, but Con was also scarred. One day had entirely changed our lives. No mention was made of a marriage proposal, and I was glad that I didn't have to add to Con's pain with a refusal at such an upsetting time.

Out of Dinny's hearing, Con raged about the Company's owners. I worried that the acid hatred he was feeling would destroy him.

"The damn robber barons have gone too far. Gram is right."

"Please, Con, stay out of the labor disputes. They're becoming violent."

"The owners think they are supreme beings, and that we're their puppets. We can't go on letting them steal from the land and the people."

I begged him to listen to me, but for the first time in our long friendship, Con would not even hear me out.

After Father's funeral, mother donated his clothing to the poor. I helped her return the borrowed furnishings used at Father's wake and give the unused supplies to other suffering families. On my last night in the patch, we attended the wakes of three men who died in the accident in which Dinny lost his legs.

One young widow was left with no means to support her

four little children. Tears poured from her red, swollen eyes in streams as she accepted condolences. Her eldest boy would be put to work in the breaker as soon as he turned eight. Until then, Mrs. McGeehan would take in laundry, sell eggs, and accept any charity that was offered. The widow was only ten years older than I, but she looked haggard in a black gown and shawl.

I left the corpse house with Wynnie, who'd also known the McGeehans. We decided to stop briefly at the Gallaghers' to visit Dinny.

"Brrr. I'm freezing. Let's cut through the alley," I said.

"Are you certain you can find your way in the dark?" asked Wynnie.

"Sure I know it like the back of my hand."

The evening was overcast, with the heavy, still atmosphere that foretells snow. When we heard a gruff male voice in the alley ahead, I began to regret taking the shortcut. Eerie snatches of disembodied conversation were coming from behind the high hedges that surrounded the Gallaghers' yard. I stopped short, trying to decide if we should stay or run back the way we came. Wynnie clutched my arm and tugged me backward, but I held a finger to my lips and leaned forward to listen.

"Our funds are scarce after all the recent calls upon them, but we'll provide Dinny with whatever we can," said a deep, rumbling voice.

"Thank you, Joe. I'll repay you as soon as I can, in cash or in kind. I don't want to be beholden." Con Gallagher! I'd know that voice anywhere. Wynnie's fingers dug into my arm so I knew she recognized our friend's voice as well.

"If you can't depend on your own people, who can you depend on?" asked the man named Joe. I couldn't make out Con's response.

"Your grandmother was right when she called us cowards. The operators have done us dirt for years, and the men aren't going to take it any more," said Joe.

"William Wight and the mine owners are inhuman. I hate every living one of them. Can you believe they charged us for the supplies used at the scene of Dinny's accident?"

"Bastards. Justice will be served, Con."

The last words were chilling in their tone.

Wynnie and I were freed from our fear-stricken immobility when we heard the two men move toward the Gallaghers' house. Wynnie started sobbing in terror. Now that we could move, I realized my feet were numb from standing on the frozen ground. Wynnie and I stumbled down the alley toward my house where we warmed up and whispered about what we heard. It certainly sounded like Con was in cahoots with Joe McDermott. I made Wynnie swear to keep the conversation a secret.

Even though it was a bleak time at home, I hated to leave the Patch, but I couldn't risk my job by staying another day. As I was no longer truly needed, I packed my bag and said tearful good-byes to my mother and sisters. Sarah and Maymie promised to write as often as possible.

As the coach rumbled down the road, I looked back at my sisters waving their handkerchiefs in farewell. The long trip to Hazleton gave me plenty of time with my thoughts. I worried that Sarah and Maymie would have to leave school to balance the family budget. Then I thought about the scroll of paper that I tucked into Father's hand in the casket. I was determined to keep my promise to take care of the family.

CHAPTER 13

Con's Connections

Each morning I cleaned the main rooms of the mansion and laid the fires in the fireplaces. I always tore out important articles from the previous day's newspapers before rolling them up for kindling. Sometimes items were already missing, having been cut out by Mr. Pardee to send to his sons. I always scanned the pages for news from Big Mine Hill or Tamaqua.

My eyes widened as I saw a letter to the editor by Joe McDermott, the labor agitator who was leading Con into dangerous intrigue. McDermott's angry opinion was sure to spark outrage in the opposing camp.

> *Editor,*
> *Your paper continually rebukes the Irish community in the region for lack of support for the Union cause, but you never take into account the sacrifices made by the Irish in the war. No one mentions the Irishmen recruited from towns like St. Clair and Port Carbon. If you check the rolls, you will see names*

like Donovan, Brennan, Dougherty and McHugh. In fact, Irishmen made up a goodly percentage of the men recruited for the Three Months' Campaign.

Why should the Irish bear the burden of fighting the Rebs when we are reviled by the very public we serve? Just four months ago, when "Paddy Owen's regulars" marched off to war through Philadelphia, they were pelted with bricks and trash because of Irish Catholic prejudice. Among these 69th Pennsylvania Volunteers were Irishmen of Schuylkill County.

Until fair practices are used by owners like Tower, Heckscher, and Pardee, we will fight conscription in every way possible. Laborers will stand together for our rights since no one else is watching out for them.

Joseph X. McDermott
Shenandoah

I hurried into the study and checked that day's paper for any rebuttal of McDermott's letter. Sure enough, Benjamin Bannan, the *Journal* editor, answered with a scorching editorial about the treasonous behavior of protesters and the knowledge and right thinking of the owners.

In part he said, "You labor agitators and Democratic Copperheads would like to see Pottsville and the Union laid in ashes. The men of the coal region, including the disloyal Irish, must serve this country to save the Union. The mine owners are proper in their enforcement of draft compliance. The interests and rights of the laboring men are under the good care of Christian men whom the wise and merciful Creator has ordained to control the property interests of our great nation."

Unrest in the mines and anti-draft activities centered in Schuylkill county, and the owners there intended to squash the rebellion and protect their own interests. My family and friends lived in Schuylkill and nearby Carbon or Luzerne counties. The coal region had many immigrants who were recruited to work the mines. All of them were subject to the draft.

As I replaced the paper on Mr. Pardee's desk, I noticed a letter placed next to a *Miner's Journal* article about the Molly Maguires. Curious, but feeling a bit guilty, I peeked at the letter and saw it was addressed to Charles Heckscher, a New Yorker who owned several mines south of Hazleton. As my eyes skimmed the letter, the name "Con Gallagher" jumped off the page. My heart thumped as I read:

> *My Dear Charles,*
> *Thank you for warning about the imminent attack on the coalfields by the forces of the Rebellion. We seem to have our hands full these days with the difficulty of wildcat strikes, the Confederates seeking to stop the coal supply to Union factories, and Mr. Lincoln's draft.*
> *About the latter concern, I have supplied a list of names of able-bodied men who are employed at my holdings in Hazleton and the surrounding vicinity. vicinity. Never let it be said that the coal region did not do its part in protecting the republic.*

When you next speak to Mr. Bannan, tell him we support his cause and will deliver the men he needs.

While those who know me refer to me as "Silent Ario," in this matter I will be vocal.

I was not aware that these secret Irish groups were so well-supplied with weaponry. I have heard of the Buckshots and the Molly Maguires, but shrugged off the matter because it seemed they were interested only in revenge against their direct superiors. I had no idea that they were so dangerous. Has Bannan informed the governor and Secretary Stanton that the groups are capable of putting 3000 men in the field on short notice? I suspect that they may cause some conflict at the railway station when the troop cars depart.

From the information I received, I believe that the prime offender is a former mine laborer named Joe McDermott. His work supervisor reported crude threats in the form of coffin notices after he was removed from his position in the mine. The man holds sway over the Irish community through his position as a political delegate. Helping him is a young fellow named Con Gallagher. Gallagher is especially dangerous because he gives fiery speeches which stir up the population. His grandmother also must be silenced.

> *We may need to request troops to be*
> *sent to maintain order.*
> *If they rid the region of these labor*
> *agitators, so much the better.*
>
> > *Respectfully yours,*
> > *Ario Pardee*

I rubbed my hand over my forehead. Con, a ringleader in the Mollies? How was it that I grew up in the Patch and never knew of the Molly Maguires? And now Mrs. Gallagher was targeted for punishment. This was worse than I imagined.

Heckscher would benefit from the removal of McDermott, Con, and other labor activists. He would use any means possible, even shooting them as trespassers at the railway station. I didn't want anyone to die, especially my friends from the Patch. Something must be done.

I impulsively considered taking the letter and burning it, but its disappearance would be noticed. I couldn't let such a dangerous message be sent. It was horrible to think of the Gallaghers being arrested, or worse.

The bold idea that lit up my brain was more of an impulse than an actual plan. I opened the center drawer of the massive desk and slipped out a piece of Pardee's monogrammed paper. Just as I slid the drawer closed, steps sounded in the hallway and the crystal doorknob turned. Glory be!

I flew across the room and slid the paper under a footed tray on the small mahogany table near the fireplace. When Mr. Pardee entered the room, I was busy dusting and polishing, all the while thinking madly. How was I going to retrieve that sheet of paper? Protocol demanded that proper servants exit the study if the master occupied the room. I'd have to curtsy and leave in a minute. What should I do?

Mr. Pardee was preoccupied with slitting open an envelope from the pile of correspondence on his desk. As the light glinted on the silver letter opener, a vague plan formed in my buzzing mind.

I began to collect all the silver items in the room as if I were going to polish them in the butler's pantry. I picked up several small silver notions and placed them on top of the tray with quavering fingers. Now I had a reason to remove the tray and the paper beneath. I moved toward the door, holding the paper securely under the bottom.

Just as I reached for the knob, I heard Mr. Pardee say, "Girl!" in a stern manner. My heart stopped for a few seconds and then restarted with a heavy thump. He walked directly toward me. I stared wide-eyed as he approached. I nearly collapsed with relief when he dropped a small silver cigar cutter onto the tray and turned away.

"Thank you, sir," I murmured and slipped out of the study. After I turned down the stairs to the butler's pantry, I slumped against the wall, weak-kneed. I heard my father's voice echoing in my head, as he cautioned me with one of his favorite sayings. "Katie, me girl, God is good, but never dance in a small boat." Somehow I'd escaped without overturning the boat.

My next step entailed forging a letter to Heckscher to keep him from enacting his plan. I didn't have much time to plan. How could I forge a letter when I didn't have a copy of Pardee's handwriting?

Wait - I wouldn't need Pardee's. I had a copy of his secretary's penmanship! I still had the letter sent to me by Jabez Williams when I was hired. I'd have to copy it over and over on butcher paper until I got it right. I only had one sheet of paper with Pardee's letterhead so my first attempt had to be perfect. In seven years of schooling I had learned how to compose a formal letter. I also had an idea of Williams's speech style and could use that to write a convincing note. Now what exactly to say...

I slipped the envelope addressed to Heckscher from the mail tray in the hallway and replaced it with my forgery. Once I had completed the exchange, I felt a little less anxious. Even if I did not stop the violence entirely I would protect my friend, Con, from immediate retribution. I needed to warn him that people were aware of his involvement in the draft protest.

I wrote a letter to Wynnie to find out what was happening in the Patch. Ever since the night we heard Con and McDermott in the alley, I dreaded hearing of any incidents related to labor organizing or the draft. On the other hand, it was all I was interested in hearing about.

> *Dear Wynnie,*
>
> *I hope you are well and recovered from the scare you suffered on the night of Joe McGeehan's wake. I often think about you and all my friends in the Patch. My sisters try to keep me up to date on the events in the area, but young girls are kept from knowing most of the unsettling news.*
>
> *Has the labor unrest continued? I try to read the paper to find out what is happening, but small town news does not always reach Hazleton. I have been terribly anxious about Con's involvement with the rough elements in the Panther Creek Valley. Please try to talk some sense into him. The authorities and owners are aware that he is involved. He may be arrested if he continues to met with McDermott.*
>
> *Is Dinny recovering? How are his spirits these days? Deirdre and Mrs.*

Gallagher give him the best of care, but
but I know from experience how much a
a man loses when he cannot work and
must depend heavily on the women in
his family.
    Is Jill settled into her new teaching
position at Owl Creek? Tell her that if
she can instruct me in tatting, she will
do wonders with her young charges.
Seeing a friend from the Patch fulfill
her dreams gives me much needed hope.
Please extend my affectionate greetings to
your family.

                 Fondly,
                 Katie

On the way to mail my letter, I ran into Patrick who was headed to McGinty's. His easy smile emboldened me to ask a favor.

"Pat, I'm terribly worried that my friend from home is going to be arrested, or worse. Con is caught in the clutches of the draft protesters. Please, will you listen around the taverns and the men's societies to find out what's happening?"

Patrick was a member of the Ancient Order of Hibernians and heard all the gossip. As an Irish speaker, Patrick was friendly with the inner circle. I knew it was bold to ask him such a big favor, but I was desperate to find out what was being planned.

"Now Katie..."

"Please Patrick, no one will tell me anything, and I feel like someone is scouring away at my insides with a scrub brush."

"Katie, Katie, Katie, you know how things are. I'd be shunned if they thought I was running my mouth after meetings."

"I know what happens to informers. I'm only asking you because I'm desperate. Con's been sucked into a bog of conspiracy, and I fear for his life."

"Say I culled some hearsay about your friend. What would you do with it."

Taking advantage of his weakening I said, "Oh thank you, thank you, I knew you'd help."

"Wait a minute. I didn't promise anything. Tell me what you would do to change your friend's mind."

"I haven't made any progress talking to Con, but I'll try to enlist Con's friends in the Patch to get him a job outside the coal region. He has cousins in Philadelphia, New York, and Wisconsin, and his grandmother has many connections. I didn't want to upset her while she was preoccupied with Dinny's injury, but Con has run amok. When she hears the story she'll take him in hand."

"Well, I'll try to help, but people will find it strange that I am suddenly concerned with draft resistance."

"I have an idea! I'll come with you to the tavern and listen in myself. That will be less dangerous for you."

"My God, Katie! Women don't frequent taverns. What's gotten into you?"

"I won't go as myself, of course. I'll borrow men's clothing and go as a groom who was hired at the stables. You'll just have to introduce me to the men as someone with a chip on his shoulder. I'll say I was blacklisted from the colliery for speaking out against the war and the draft."

"Don't you know how dangerous this could be? Some of these men talk of violent methods to get justice. Some of it's just the bottle talking, but injustice mixed with the Drink makes for an explosive mixture."

"Just think about it, please?"

"I can't imagine changing my mind, but I'll think about it."

CHAPTER 14

Cajoling Patrick

Pat ducked away from my anxious gaze every time I passed him in the kitchen or yard. He knew I was still angling to go to McGinty's. I was as jumpy as a rasher of bacon on a hot griddle. Somehow I had to set a plan into action.

In late April, while returning from an errand, I overheard the men discussing the May Day bonfire. Immigrants from the rural glens of County Donegal still celebrated the May first rituals that marked Beltane, a festival of the old ways. The men from McGinty's would gather at the celebration. Whiskey and ale flowed at such events.

I cornered Patrick at the earliest opportunity.

"I want you to take me to the lighting of the belfire on April 30," I told him.

"Katie, no! That's an even worse idea than going to McGinty's! We'd be up in the woods for much of the night, away from help if anything went wrong. And there's a lot that could go wrong."

"Pat, I must go. The papers tell me only so much, but I know the situation is reaching a crisis. I need to hear with my own ears what McDermott is planning."

"There'll be drinking and carrying on, and language not fit for your ears! What would your mother say about that?"

"She and my father, God rest him, would be glad I was taking a stand for my friend. But if you won't take me, I'll find another way." I set my chin and stared at him, waiting for his decision.

"You're the most stubborn article I ever met." Pat kicked at the edge of a flagstone and fretted his cap as he weighed my words. A shout came from the coachhouse for Patrick to hitch the carriage. Pressed for time and knowing my determination, Pat grudgingly agreed to help.

The night of the bonfire, I opened the burlap sack of clothes that Patrick had given me and began to transform myself into a stable boy. I bound my upper body using sheets and sashes from my dresses. Thank goodness I was tall for a girl.

I added walnut juice to Old Mrs. Gallagher's cold cream recipe and rubbed the mixture on my face. As I breathed in the fresh cucumber smell of the cream, memories of the Gallaghers' house flooded back.

With the slight darkening of my skin, some stippling of soot on my jaw, and the bulky wrappings, I looked like a stocky lad in need of a shave. I twisted my braids under a soft slouch hat and made my way out to the stableyard.

It was fortunate that the master and his family were away that last day of April since the various celebrations lasted into the night. Attendees often greeted the morning with a sore head. Most of the female staff had gone to the tamer park festivities hours earlier.

Patrick glanced up, and a prickle of excitement shot through me when I saw his face. A stunned stare replaced the blank look. My confidence soared as I strode across the flagstones, mimicking the swagger of Con Gallagher.

"Dominick Harkins, at your service," I said.

"Don't talk until we leave the Square," Pat warned as he threw straw and clean blankets in the back of the wagon. His jerky movements and gruff voice dampened my enthusiasm a bit, but if my disguise was good enough to fool Pat in the full light of day, it would be perfect on a dark hillside with only flickering light from the fire.

Pat and I headed to the countryside west of Hazleton, to the high acres looming over the neat patchwork of Conyngham Valley farms. After driving a few miles, my companion warmed up enough to point out some landmarks. I gasped as the wagon rounded a bend. I'd never seen Sugarloaf Mountain where the bel fire would be set. The amazing peak rose like a mound of cocoa in the bowl-shaped valley. In a few weeks the brown hill would be clothed in soft green.

We bounced and jolted the last few miles. After leaving the main pike, we traveled on roads that were little more than cowpaths. Ravines formed by spring flooding made travel on the rugged trail dangerous. One wagon wheel lurched into a hole and nearly overset us. Seeing the sheer drop alongside the path made my stomach flip, then land with a thud.

It was not completely dark, but the sun had dipped beneath the mountains by the time we met up with the Hibernians.

"Hey, lads, pull your rig over there, away from the pathway." Pat followed the orders. We unhitched the horses to allow them to graze while we headed to the blazing bonfire. I was glad my disguise passed inspection in daylight because the light of the flames was surprisingly bright. Our lanterns paled in comparison.

Pat introduced me to several of the younger men clustered on rough log benches, laughing and talking. The language of the group was peppered with swear words, but I didn't flinch, though my ears burned at some of the vulgar jokes. I didn't understand much of the humor though there was one story that I knew would be enjoyed by Gram and Aunt Aggie.

The burly fellow telling the joke cleared his throat and began: God was busy working on the creation of the Earth when St. Michael the Archangel came up and asked what he was making.

God replied, "It's another planet, but I'm after putting LIFE on this one. I've named it Earth and there's going to be a balance between everything on it. For example, there's going to be some rich parts and an equal number of poor parts. There's going to be hot places and cold places.

And then the archangel said, "and what's that green dot there?" And God said, "That's the Emerald Isle - a very special place. That's going to be the most glorious spot on earth. The people there are going to be great jokesters and travelers. They'll be playwrights and poets and singers and songwriters. And I'm going to give them this black liquid which they're going to go mad on and for which people will come from the far corners of the earth to imbibe."

At this point the crowd cheered and hoisted their glasses. "Ahh boys, that's unfortunately not where the story ends," said Tim with mock sadness. "Michael the Archangel gasped in admiration at the beautiful island, but then frowned, asking: "But what will balance out all those good things?"

God replied, "Ahh, wait until you see the neighbors I'm going to give them!"

The crowd cheered and slapped the man on the back. The men passed a jug of poteen and visited the barrel of ale, filling all manner of containers with the sharp-smelling brew. I felt I was holding my own until I saw a familiar face across the circle. Fragments of memory flashed through my mind until I realized it was Felty, the delivery man from McGrogan's, who often came to the servants' entrance with Cook's order of fresh fish and oysters.

Suddenly the seriousness of my masquerade hit me, and my confidence sifted away like cold ashes though a grate. Did I look familiar to him? Did he recognize me? I suddenly felt exposed.

Pat saw me shift in my seat and asked if I wanted to move closer to the fire. I shook my head no. The gruff voice I was using quavered, and a few times I had to clear my voice before starting to speak so I just sat back and listened. My heartbeat drummed in my ears, muffling sound so just following the conversation became difficult.

After a while I became a wee bit more comfortable since everyone seemed to accept my story at face value, and Felty had not approached us. The conversation was cheerful social chatter, not the serious plotting I expected. It was not much different from the after dinner sessions at the Square. The stories were amusing, but I was beginning to believe my efforts were wasted until Pat and I moved to the far side of the clearing. There we found ourselves among the hard-nosed political group. As we got closer to the fire, I turned my back to the flames. My former confidence was eroded by a newfound fear - that my make-up would melt.

"Pat, me boyo, glad you made it," a familiar gruff voice said. That voice chilled my blood and brought back the memory of the alley behind the Gallaghers. Its distinctive edge, as well as the fear it incited in me months ago, made it very memorable. Joe McDermott, in the flesh.

Other voices chimed in, and I tried to put names to the faces, but it was difficult in the flickering firelight. Suddenly I was the center of attention as Pat introduced me.

"Joe, this is Dominick Harkins, a new hire at Pardee Square."

"Pleased to meet yeh, sir." I deepened my voice and kept my handshake firm as I greeted McDermott and the other men.

"How do you come to be in hard coal country, Dominick?" asked Big Joe. I started at the sound of my "name." I'd gotten comfortable sitting in the background, but now I was back in the thick of things.

"Me and my mam came up from Allentown about ten years

ago," I said. "I worked in the southern field until I was blacklisted by an S.O.B. of a boss. Mam passed away from consumption last summer so I came up here.

"Blacklisted, eh? Same as meself." I sensed his approval and took advantage.

"Blacklisted for being Irish?" I asked.

"No, the boss dinna like hearing the truth. The bastard was abusing the trust of a poor slow boy who couldn't learn to add for a hill of beans. Kline was shorting the lad's car every time he came for a weigh-in. I caught Kline at his chicanery and got poor Jimmy Touchie his fair wage, but I was fired the next day and never got another job in the area. 'Twas the death of me noble dream of being a mine baron," Joe laughed dryly. "I'd do the same thing agin, though. And yerself?"

I recited the story Pat and I had concocted about being unfairly treated at the Mount Laffee mine. The men nodded while I told the story since it was a rather common one, and then attention turned to other matters. I relaxed my hunched shoulders and listened.

Eventually the talk turned to the war and the draft. This was what I was waiting for, but I did not want to seem too eager.

"How many men from the western area can we pull together to protest the draft, McGee?" asked McDermott.

"I'd say about a hundred," said McGee.

"How staunch are these men? Are they ready to take a beating for the cause?" McDermott asked.

"They're sick of the poor treatment they're getting from the bosses so I think we can depend on them standing solid."

"What about Carbon and the east, Devers?"

"We have more than a hundred, but some are family men and they might be swayed by their women. Several are already talking about moving west with the railroad."

"Last week at McGinty's, Edward Clarke from Shenandoah reported that Charlemagne Tower and Bannan were enraging the residents of their county by unfair procedures and propaganda against the Irish."

"What's going to be done about it?" asked one of Big Joe's buddies.

"Everyone in the back room discussed our options. Dan here will tell you all about it."

"One idea is to protest by having a work stoppage on the day of the draft. Another is to apply to the courts for exemptions of men who are sole breadwinners and those who are not citizens. Clarke suggested blowing up the train tracks in advance of the train so it can't leave the station. He would also like to send threats to Tower's estate warning him to stay out of this business and mind his own."

"Can't we set up a fund to send away the men who don't want to go to war?"

"The problem is money. No one has enough to hire a lawyer to fight in court, and no one has fare money for all the men who choose not to fight to leave the region."

"Either way there'll be money trouble. The benevolent society won't be able to help all the families who'll need help if the breadwinners are sent to war."

"Can we can steal enough powder to blow up the tracks?" asked Big Joe.

"We'll be up for a federal charge if we use black powder and get caught," said Dan.

"Ní bhíonn bua mór gan contúirt," said Joe.

I nudged Patrick who translated, "There is never a great victory without danger."

"Who's in if we decide to blow up the tracks so the train can't leave?" asked Joe.

Several men volunteered immediately while others held back, not wanting to get involved in such a big operation. We were huddled together in a rough circle, speaking in low but serious tones.

When Pat heard me say, "I'm in, Joe," his arm twitched, then stiffened against mine. A few moments later he muttered, "Count me in, too."

Poor chivalrous Patrick. I'm sure he regretted coming.

Several more voices expressed opinions, but no conclusion was reached. Speech became garbled as the night advanced and the men, who had been drinking for several hours, were becoming rowdy. Songs and jokes replaced serious talk.

As we were leaving, Pat stopped to say good-bye to the younger men. Felty, the delivery man, pulled him aside. It appeared that Pat was laughing off something he said. Pat gave Felty a friendly shove, then climbed into the wagon.

"What was that all about?" I asked once Pat was settled into the driver's seat.

"Twas none of your concern." Pat's voice and manner made me wonder why he was lying, but asking him was only throwing ink on a black sky. I felt like saying, "Who's the stubborn article now?" But Patrick was stiff and silent with disapproval.

"This is not a lark, Catharine," was his only comment.

Tired and aching, I lapsed into sleep, but lurched awake whenever we hit a rut. Back at the Square, I rubbed the make-up from my face with plain grease and rags, then splashed my cheeks with cold water and collapsed into bed. I only had two hours of sleep before I needed to be up to light the fires downstairs.

During the third week of May, Patrick spotted me outside the kitchen door, working on my own. His spoke to me in a hushed tone which held a note of aggravation.

"Joe McDermott is holding a meeting in McGinty's back room on Thursday. I've been told to inform you, *Dominick*. Now what?" Patrick was still annoyed that I wrangled him into my masquerade.

"Lord, I can't make it to a meeting on Thursday night! You know how cantankerous Mrs. Lane gets when guests are due to arrive."

The Pardees were entertaining a weekend party of city friends so I knew I could not attend the meeting, but I begged Patrick to go and keep me informed.

I did not get an opportunity to speak to Patrick until Vespers on Sunday evening. I sidled up to Pat on the way out of St. Gabriel's. Some young ladies who had their eyes on the handsome bachelor gave me disdainful glances, but I ignored their snubs. Let them think I had romantic intentions. It was good cover for our murmured conversation.

Patrick reported that McDermott's plan to stop the train by blowing up the tracks was going forward even though a large group of Hibernians decided not to support him.

The moderate group, led by Tinker Ward, was trying to convince a politician to support their cause for a peaceful resolution to the conflict. Calm reasoning was increasingly difficult now that Pennsylvanians faced the grim results of war.

The casualties were returning to coal country daily, both bodies and the injured. Some of the injuries were hideous, and the bodies, shipped in cheap wooden caskets, were often unrecognizable. Burial was immediate, without the traditional wake, due to the advanced decomposition of the dead. Grieving parents, wives, and sweethearts had only their memories to sustain them. Amputations left some survivors hobbling on crutches. Others were left with empty sleeves and empty futures.

The early victories of the South had fired up Washington and the battles became bloodier and more furious...

CHAPTER 15

Conscription

Other than Patrick, the only person who knew of my secret mission was Wynnie. I could not burden my sisters. Sarah and Maymie wrote to me weekly, but I never told them of my worries. They showed my letters to Mother and would never keep secrets from her. Mother would tell Gram and Aunt Aggie. I did not want anyone to fret or try to talk me out of my plans. I certainly did not want rumors to leak out in the Patch. I knew I could trust Wynnie. She stood at my side that February night when McDermott entrapped Con, playing on his raw emotions. Wynnie understood.

The sealed envelope containing my friend's latest letter was in my pocket, and it crackled as I walked. I could barely wait to slit it open. When I reached the privacy of my room, a stained rectangle of newsprint slipped out with the letter.

> *My Dear Friend,*
> *I hope this note finds you well and safe. The situation that is worrying both of us has worsened. Our friend from the west side of town has been gone for the past two weeks, and his mother and grandmother are haggard*

with worry. The local bosses won't hire him as a day laborer because of his politics. It is accepted as common knowledge that he's in cahoots with the Mollies. If you learn anything of his whereabouts, please let me know.

Dinny has healed wonderfully. He is getting around on a special cart made for him by Farmer Zern. Old Mrs. Gallagher cured Zern's wife and he wanted to repay the favor. Dinny's natural agility and strength have served him well. Con's bitterness dampened his twin's spirits, but Dinny knows nothing about Con's quest for vengeance. He only knows that Con is gone. We are all hiding our worry.

Your Sarah is helping Jill at the schoolhouse in exchange for tutoring in mathematics. She is learning natural science by helping Mrs. Gallagher mix medicine, too. You were right about her ability. She is so bright and hardworking. I see young Maymie only when she stops in the shop after school. She buzzes with energy, that one.

I know how interested you are in the political events down the line. While I was wrapping a leg of mutton in butcher paper and newsprint, I saw this article about Charlemagne Tower and the unrest in Heckscher's

*mines. Tower is using the troops to
further his own interests at the cost
of poor laborers. Did you hear that
he is strong-arming all the local
operators to give up their employment
lists so he can exceed his draft quotas?
He wants to enlist every man between
the ages of 20 and 45, regardless of
citizenship status or other exceptions.
There are many men who are
misrolled. Now there are many who
will never come back.*

    *We had word from Philadelphia
that Annie O'Donnell's brother died
of wounds he sustained at the Battle
of Malvern Hill in July. The heavy
guns caused huge casualties, possibly
5,000 were killed. God willing, this
terrible war will be over soon.*

              Yours,
              Wynnie

Johnny O'Donnell, dead. Tears welled as I thought of the
O'Donnell clan. Annie's family left the coal region for
Philadelphia to escape the dangers of the mines, but they lost
Johnny anyway.

Johnny O. was held up as a model to his younger cousins,
Con and Dinny, but they never resented him. He was always
willing to help the boys with their school assignments or fishing
skills. Johnny either had a book in his hands or a fishing rod.
My heart was sore as I recalled seeing him at his desk, his pale
serious face focused on a Latin passage in the catechism book.
Johnny's mother had great hopes that he would enter the
priesthood. Another shattered dream. Another reason for Con
to hate the war.

I wiped my eyes and picked up the item that had slipped from the folds of the note - a clipping from the *Journal*.

"Miners Threaten Operations" blared across the top. Charlemagne Tower, the Provost Marshall, had his hands full in the Cass Township area. The miners threatened to flood the mines by turning off the pumps. Hatred that had been simmering for decades boiled to the surface.

Bannan and Tower blamed the Irish Democrats for Franklin Pierce's victory. Now they were taking revenge. Tower reported to officials in Harrisburg that there were three thousand men ready to take up arms against the draft.

Three thousand? Lordy, where did Tower get that outlandish figure? McDermott had not managed to gather a tenth of that number despite a combination of cajoling and heavy-handed threats. I tucked the clipping into my apron pocket and went to the stables to show Patrick.

After reading the article, he said, "Tower is stretching the numbers so that the military becomes a fixture in the coal regions."

"Why?"

"Tower's and Heckscher's interests are protected by the armed troops. It solves their problems if labor leaders get arrested as agitators of civil unrest."

"Will the troops convince McDermott not to try anything?"

"No, McDermott is just as ripe for action as the miners are. He plans to stop the draft train at Tremont and release any men who have not volunteered. The newest plan is to have his men create a diversion so that some of the troops are drawn away from the station.'"

"When was this decided?"

"Last week at McGinty's."

I placed my hands on my hips and challenged Patrick. "Why didn't you tell me about the plan?"

Patrick's brow crinkled, and he bristled like an angry

hound. "I hoped you would come to your senses and stay out of this."

"At least I could have attended the meeting!"

"I didn't tell you about it because Felty Carroll from McGrogan's asked if you were coming. He's been curious about you ever since Beltane."

"I noticed him frowning at me on the night of the bonfire, but I didn't think he recognized me as a maid from the mansion." I closed my eyes, trying to remember. "Whenever he delivered Cook's order, I opened the door and greeted him. He teased me about my sparkling Irish eyes."

"Felty made a joke about Dominick's weak head for alcohol as we left the gathering that night. He noticed you weren't drinking with the rest of the men," said Patrick.

"How did you explain my absence from last week's meeting?"

"I told him that both of us couldn't leave the stables at the same time when the Pardees were in town, but he senses a flam."

"Let him suspect."

"Please Katie, if Felty discovers your plan and reports it to McDermott, your life is forfeit."

"I'll stay out of Felty's way when he delivers the oysters, but I'm not going to be put off," I said. "So, when are they stopping the train?"

Pat shrugged when he saw I was set on my decision. "McDermott plans to be ready for the first train to leave the station with draftees. We're meeting again tomorrow night."

I gasped to fill my lungs. Oh, for a breath of breeze! The heat spell was unusual for the heights of Hazleton, especially in September. My hot, airless attic room was bad enough when I was wearing my uniform, but with the extra wrappings of the disguise, the heat was excruciating. I peered into my hand mirror to dab on more cold cream mixture before leaving to meet with Big Joe at Bach's hotel in the village of Audenreid, junction of the three coal counties.

The other servants' bedrooms were empty. The heat wave had forced everyone to cooler locations. The moonless night helped my secret mission a little too. Even though we were leaving Hazleton, there was a chance of seeing Felty or someone else I knew.

On the trip south, Patrick spouted all manner of directions. He was as fidgety as a broody hen on Easter morning. Stay in the background. Speak only if necessary. Follow my lead.

Taking orders galled me, but I bit my tongue and nodded. When I had the chance to speak my piece, I told Patrick he should volunteer to transport the powder before someone else got the job. It was important that we be in the thick of things.

He huffed and bluffed, but eventually gave in. I wished I had such control over Con. Then we would not be in this dangerous position.

Bach's was a German drinking establishment frequented by the Irish. The dark interior was hazy with smoke and heat, but I could make out a small cluster of men seated with their backs to the door. I strolled toward the table with Pat at my back, squinting to identify Joe among the men.

Pat bumped into me as I rocked back on my heels at the sight of a familiar black cowlick. I blinked twice, but the sight remained the same. Con Gallagher! So this is where he has been. Patrick frowned and shot me a questioning look, but there was no way to inform him of the problem. Sweat popped out on my forehead and hands. My only hope was to stay clear of Con's line of vision.

Greetings accompanied the scraping of chairs as we joined the group. Con glanced at us but seemed more interested in the conversation of the man on his right. His brow was wrinkled in concentration, but when he smiled a familiar grin crinkled his eyes and bracketed his mouth. When McDermott ordered a round of pints, I placed my hand over the glass to keep the bartender from filling it. Big Joe leaned across Patrick to peer at me.

"I have trouble trustin' a fella who doesn't drink," said McDermott.

I knew my abstinence from drinking would be noticed so I had my reason prepared. "I took the pledge." My words seemed to linger, suspended in the air. "On her deathbed my mother asked me to swear I wouldn't drink, and in her honor I keep my word."

"Well, Father Mathew's temperance campaign is not for me at all, at all. But I have to give credit where it's due." He lifted his glass in recognition. "In any case, I'll be drinkin' enough for both of us." He roared with laughter and tossed down the ale. "Yeh know what they say, 'Drink is the curse of the land. It makes you fight with your neighbor. It makes you shoot at your landlord, and it makes you miss him.'"

Another great gulder shook his shoulders. Joe was in fine humor this evening.

"Now boys, it's time for some serious discussion. Beggin' your pardon to the young lads, but this subject is too important for English. Half the drinkers here only speak Dutchie, but it's best to switch to Irish."

That was an unexpected reprieve. Using a husky voice and staying out of Con's sight would have been a challenge. The conversation was rapid and hushed, but I was able to pick up a word of Irish here and there. The last instruction was in English. Share the word with all bodies of Mollies in the patches and villages of the surrounding counties. Patrick translated the rest on the ride home.

Joe's plan was to steal small quantities of powder and assemble the ingredients to blow up the railroad tracks in Tremont. Laborers from the thirty collieries in the area would be needed to steal enough powder. Then someone would take the supplies to Pottsville and pass them off to the men there. Members would be positioned in Pottsville, Orwigsburg, and Tamaqua as well as the Tremont location. Death threatened any man who thwarted the gang.

Mail was delivered to Pardee Square at three, and I always took my break at that time. Peering into the pigeonhole and seeing mail was the highlight of my day. I pulled out three envelopes and turned them over in my hands, savoring the anticipation. I smiled as I recognized the first two - Aunt Aggie and my sister Sarah. The third was different. It was not Wynnie's hand, nor was it from Mother or Gram. They would never send such a grubby letter.

James, standing in the doorway, saw my confusion. "That didn't come with the regular delivery."

My brows snapped together. "How then?"

"A young scamp trotted up to the service gate and gave it to Tweeny. She passed it to me, and I put it there since I know check your mail every day."

"Thank you, James."

I took the letters out to the bench in the courtyard and started with Sarah's note. My sister was not the best correspondent. She was too kind to write any of the interesting gossip.

On the other hand, Aunt Aggie's tight upright hand lambasted everyone in the Patch, especially her enemies across the lane, the Brennans. Her usual complaints and warnings overflowed the page, but the cautions held an undercurrent of caring that I had finally begun to appreciate.

The third letter was a curiosity. The envelope had been turned inside out for reuse. It had once held someone's pay from the Springbrook Colliery. The original addressee was scratched out and "C. McCafferty" was scrawled across the front. I slit open the envelope and pulled out a sheet of cheap lined paper. A strong pen stroke leapt across the smudged page.

> *We now about yer tricks.*
> *Stop this mummery or we*
> *will out you to the big man.*
> *A friend*

Someone knew about my masquerade as Dominick. Who? I examined the note and envelope for an answer.

Patrick? Trying to scare me from my plan? No, he would just find a way to stop me. He warns me every time we are alone.

Con? Did he recognize me the other night? He did not seem to suspect anything. If he recognized me, he would have found a way to locate me and warn me off in person.

Felty, the oyster delivery man? Again, why a note? He had no reason to protect me. He would report his suspicions to McDermott without sending me a note.

A member of McDermott's gang who recognized me from one of the meetings? If so, which one? Did someone already tell McDermott of my real identity? Was it a blackmailer hoping to frighten me and then ask for money?

I rested my head in my hands. The unnerving message rattled me.

Just then a pair of hands reached from the shrubbery behind me and touched my shoulder. I yelped in surprise.

"Patrick, why you..." I simmered with anger at revealing weakness. I detested squealing girls.

Tucking the letter into my apron, I turned to face him, but before I could give him a piece of my mind, Patrick said, "Joe's asked me to smuggle the goods to Pottsville on the next trip to pick up supplies,"

"Wonderful!" My frown turned into a grin.

"We'll see how wonderful things are if something goes wrong."

"When is the powder needed?" I asked.

"Only Joe knows the exact date and time it'll be used. Sometime after Wednesday."

"I'll take the trip with you. It'll be easy to convince Cook that she needs certain supplies that only I can choose. Anyway, she thinks I'm sweet on you and she's promoting the match."

"Lord save me from bossy women!" said Patrick.

CHAPTER 16

Conspiracy

I rolled onto my back, punched my pillow, and flung my braids aside to get comfortable. The muscles of my back and neck bunched with tension. I needed rest in order to be sharp in the morning, but sleep was impossible. After hours of frustrated tossing, I sat up and hunched over the edge of my cot and rubbed my puffy eyes. I fumbled for a match from the box beside the bed and lit a stub of candle.

I knelt beside the bed, but my prayers seemed more like striking a deal than conversing with God so I slid a prayer card from my Missal and stared at the picture of Jesus kneeling against a large rock. The Agony in the Garden.

Scenes flashed through my mind: Johnnie Pat's body being carried from the mine, my father's silent suffering, Con's pain on hearing of his brother's accident, my mother's face at Father's wake, poor Mrs. McGeehan flanked by her little sons, women meeting the military train and discovering the horror of war. Praying usually gave me a sense of peace, but solace escaped me as I knelt there in the flickering candlelight.

I rose and crossed to the ewer to splash water on my face, then dressed for the day. My motions as I performed the morning chores were like Izzy's toy soldier winding down.

Routine activities kept me occupied until noon when

Patrick came and gave Mrs. Lane Cook's note saying that I was to accompany him on a buying trip to Pottsville. With a "Humpf," Mrs. Lane nodded to me.

I removed my apron and ran up to the third floor to get my cape and bonnet. On the landing I paused to catch my breath and say a little prayer.

"Dear God, let your archangel Michael spread his wings over us and protect us from evil." I hurriedly blessed myself and ran back to the kitchen.

I accepted the list of supplies Mrs. Lane wanted for the household, then climbed onto the buckboard seat next to Pat without glancing into the box of the wagon. McDermott told Patrick to wrap the powder box in rags and hide it under some hay in the back. A shovel and pick, and a ropelike fuse for the powder were also concealed in the pile.

McDermott's orders were to take the back road over Locust Mountain to Port Carbon. Some local men would meet us and bury the goods in a shrubby area near the Schuylkill canal. We had a long trip, but the pace we kept allowed a breeze to cool us. It was a bright early autumn day and once out of the city, I began to enjoy the scenery.

"The Pennsylvania mountains, the green valleys and gray boulders remind me of Donegal," said Pat.

"Do you miss Ireland?" Somehow I had never asked him that question before.

"At times I dream of the cottage in Killybegs and wish I could see it again." Patrick's face had a distant look as if he was seeing something on the horizon.

"Do you still have family there?"

"Yes, my mother and widowed sister and some nieces and nephews are there. I'm saving to bring them over." Pat's complexion flushed with color.

"What of your father?"

"I barely remember my da'. He died when I was six, during

the Hunger. It's hard to be without a father. That's why I want to help Nora raise her children. I can teach the boys how to shoe horses. We can eventually open a blacksmith shop in town." Pat's face lit with determination.

"I'm glad you have dreams, Pat."

"As long as you work hard, dreams are possible in America."

"May they come true for both of us."

I hoped I would not shatter Patrick's dreams by getting him fired. Was I saving Con at the expense of my new friend? I sat quietly, deep in my own thoughts, for the next hour.

The mines were in full operation at every colliery along the way, meeting the needs of the monster war. Trains passing us were loaded with freight or troops heading south to replace those killed in the recent heavy fighting.

I shivered even though the day was warm. What if somehow the explosives in the wagon were discovered? Pat and I would be arrested. I shuddered at the thought of being locked up in a grim stone jailhouse.

Our meeting place was just north of the city in the former canal town. We needed to get rid of the supplies before we picked up Cook's order. Some of the blasting powder would be used to distract the troops. The remainder would be sent down river to the actual site where the train would be stopped and the consignees pulled out. Local troops looking for agitators were stationed at intervals from the eastern end of the county at Tamaqua to Pottsville.

After hours of driving, we were on the outskirts of the city. I remembered little of the surroundings from my visit last winter. Pat was knowledgeable about our route, but his posture was anything but confident. Whenever soldiers on horseback passed us, he hunched over the reins.

"Buck up, boyo, or you'll get us hanged." I nudged Patrick in the ribs.

He straightened a tad, but his face still wore a wary frown. The soldiers patrolling the territory looked edgy, and we could not afford to attract attention.

As we approached the village of Tuscarora, Pat was first to spy the roadblock. "Now we're gone and done for." His fatalist attitude mirrored my own, but I could not let Patrick see it.

No one seeing my flaming hair and freckles or Pat's ruddy complexion would mistake us for anything but Irish, and therefore suspect. Pat's slouch added to his guilty appearance. Another mark against us. Sweat trickled down my spine as I imagined the soldiers flinging out the straw and seeing the powder.

Certain wagons stopped for a few minutes, but others were searched thoroughly. Were they looking for a specific individual or just any suspicious character? I worked on a plan to distract the attention of the uniformed men from Pat's agitated appearance while we sat in the line of carts waiting for clearance. I adjusted my dress and bonnet and preened a bit.

"Hello, Officer. How are things with you this fine day?" I tossed my head and peered up into the eyes of the young man on horseback with a friendly smile.

"M'am, I'm not an officer. The commander is on the far side of the crowd."

"Oh, I thought that smart uniform and your fine mount meant that you were an officer. Begging your pardon, sir, but with your stature I'm sure it won't be long until you move up in rank. And it's miss, not m'am." I smiled to display my dimples and threw in a lighthearted flounce for good measure.

The young soldier shot a quick look at Patrick who was now looking more peeved than worried. "Thank you, miss. I sure hope you're right. But unless I'm mistaken, my captain is wondering why I am dithering here instead of doing my job."

"What is your job?" I asked innocently.

"We're looking for some dangerous men who are in the

region. This checkpoint keeps track of the people entering the city. No one comes in unless they have a need."

"Oh, we have a reason. Patrick, where's our list?"

"Here you are," said Pat, handing him Mrs. Lane's crisp supply list. "I make the trip to Pottsville for the Pardees of Hazleton once a month."

The private scanned the sheet with Pardee's letterhead on top. He asked which businesses and farms we would be visiting, and Pat rattled off the names. Everything seemed to be going smoothly until the young cavalryman focused his attention on the back of the wagon.

He leaned forward with his gun and said, "Just in case someone hid himself in your wagon box, I'd better check."

My heart jumped, and its beat thumped in my ears till I thought it would burst out of my chest. Pat was frozen beside me, and I dared not look in his direction.

The soldier flipped his rifle and began poking the bayonet into the straw. He pulled it out and dangling on the point was the coil of rope fuse.

For a moment all three of us just stared. The quizzical look on the soldier's face demanded an explanation, but all I could think of was what my family would do if I were jailed. How could we possibly explain having a fuse in the wagon?

I usually had a way with words, but right now my wits were fuddled. The background sounds of horses snorting, men shouting, and children whining were muffled vibrations clogged my mind. It seemed that the day had darkened under a passing cloud.

I felt myself sway on the seat when Pat broke the silence saying, "We're stopping at Maurer's Kennel to pick up some hound pups. Old Jacob Maurer raises the best trackers in the state. That's the rope to secure their crate in the box."

"Anderson!" The young trooper wheeled around at the bark of his commanding officer and saw some angry delivery men causing a ruckus at the rear of the line. He tossed the "rope" back into the wagon and, with a sweep of his hat, waved us on our way. When he wheeled around and moved to the rear to subdue the commotion, the spine-stiffening tension evaporated, and I trembled like one of Cook's gelatin molds. Mercy, that was close, I thought.

"I've never seen you speechless before, Katie. What happened to your well of compliments for Private Anderson? I was waiting for more feminine wiles to get us out of that pickle."

Patrick's taunts rallied my spirit. "Well, I can't be expected to do all the work on this trip. It's a darn good thing that argument broke out when it did."

Silence reigned in the wagon until we pulled off at the Port Carbon farmers' market, our meeting place. We loitered at the far edge of the field waiting for our contact, a man wheeling a barrow of turnips.

We saw him in the distance, bumping along. As he neared our wagon, we looked for the prearranged sign.

The man put the thumb of his left hand in his belt loop in a deliberate manner and said, "The nights lately have been fine."

Pat copied his hand signal and answered, "Yes, with luck we should have a good harvest."

Satisfied, the man told us to wait until the stock auction started before putting our "freight" in the wheelbarrow and taking it to the abandoned canal path where we would find a freshly dug trench. It seemed that we would be expected to bury the contraband.

We located the hole quickly and placed the black powder and other items inside, covering it over with canvas, dirt, and leaves. Pat left the area first with the barrow, now much lighter. I followed, shaking straw and cobwebs from my skirt.

I heaved a sigh as I climbed onto the well-used seat of the wagon. We exited the market and headed to the city, passing many vehicles headed for the auction. Cook's errands did not take long, and we were soon headed back across Locust Mountain to Hazleton.

Once the fear of discovery was gone, I worried that McDermott's men would use the powder before the scheduled date. What if Pat and I could not return and complete my plan? Someone might be killed as a result of my efforts to stop bloodshed, the exact opposite of what I wanted to happen. If that happened, how would I ever forgive myself?

CHAPTER 17

Cloaked Correspondence – October 3, 1862

Someone knows about Dominick. The refrain dinned in my head like the echoing church bells. Who has been watching me?

It could be anyone. Since both the Molly Maguires and the Knights of the Golden Circle were secret organizations, no one really knew who was a member.

Two more ominous notes had arrived by messenger last week. The latest one was a warning to stay away from Pottsville. As I checked the mail, I braced myself to find another grubby envelope, then sighed with relief when I did not find one. The anxiety spoiled my anticipation of news from home.

Earlier, while returning from an errand downtown, I caught myself glancing over my shoulder to see if I was being followed. Were prying eyes watching me carry out my daily chores?

I shivered and twitched the curtains aside with the feather duster as I tidied the parlor, thinking to catch a glimpse of the young messenger or some other stranger lingering around the Square. I was becoming fearful of my own shadow.

Then, as clear as day, I heard my father's calm voice saying, "If you're the only one that knows you're afraid, you're brave."

The advice stiffened my spine. I shook off my unease and whispered, "Thank you, Da'."

Letters from the Patch arrived regularly. I kept my concerns from my family, but poured them out to Wynnie in long letters. After seeing Con in Audenreid, I asked her to visit the Gallaghers to find out what they knew of Con's involvement with the protesters. I hoped I was not becoming a burden to my friend, but I could not trust anyone else.

Wynnie's letter reported that some strangers were in the Patch asking the Welsh and English miners and storekeepers about Con and his grandmother. Con was supposedly working at a bootleg mine in Honeybrook. He had not returned to the Patch since being blacklisted by the Company. Every Saturday, a laborer who boarded in Audenried during the week took Con's pay to the Gallaghers. Dinny did not even hint at knowledge of his twin's stance against the draft. Either he did not know of his brother's activities or feared talking about them.

In my last letter to Wynnie I had mentioned the mysterious unsigned messages. My friend's alarm was evident in the question, "What if Con recognized you and gave away your identity to the others?"

I shook my head as I read. Con would never be so cold-hearted. Hotheaded, yes, but never unfeeling. As I continued reading, Wynnie's meaning became clear: Con, in his surprise, might have betrayed me. I briefly considered that idea, but dismissed it. That night at Bach's Hotel, he showed no reaction to my presence whatsoever.

At least the author of the messages had not attempted anything dangerous. Yet.

Certainly bravery was needed in our troubled times. The headlines in the dailies screamed "Violence and Pillage," "The Ferocities of the Mob," and "Militia Shoots into Crowd" as rioting spread across the North. The enrollment met strong resistance, especially among the immigrant populations of Wisconsin, Maryland, and the mining and agricultural regions of our state. Protesters of the draft jeered that it was "a rich man's war, but a poor man's fight." I knew McDermott must be ready to make his move.

Two weeks after our trip to Schuylkill County, Patrick signaled to me from the stable, and I met him out by the garden bench.

"Big Joe was pleased with our performance in Port Carbon. He said we proved ourselves ready to make the trip south for the big event."

"When and where exactly?" The time was near, and I was anxious to finish my task, safely, God willing. Who knows what would happen to all of us afterwards.

"The train of draftees will depart from Pottsville on the sixteenth, and most of the militia will be expecting trouble at the station. Some protesters will be there to create a distraction, but most of the men will be posted on the southern tracks ready to set off the explosion and release the drafted men."

I heard the slam of the kitchen screen door and saw Tweeny coming out for some fresh air. Patrick and I hurriedly finished our discussion and arranged to meet before sunrise on the designated day.

CHAPTER 18

Carrying Out The Plan

October 16 was cool and damp. The horses seemed to sense my jittery mood and clattered their hooves against the cobbled drive. Vapor wreathed their heads as they snorted in anticipation of the coming trip. Patrick hitched them up and stowed the heavy wooden box in the wagon, then tossed me the bag of men's clothing. I would play the role of Dominick for the last time.

"Katie, stay away from the lead group today. Felty Carroll and McDermott will be in that crowd."

"I may not be able to avoid them. If Con is with McDermott, that's where I'll be."

Pat hunched his shoulders and swung his head from side to side like a contrary mule, but he did not argue the point.

We had to take some rough roads in order to reach the meeting place between Pottsville and Tower City in time. Thick fog delayed our progress, and I squirmed on the wagon bench.

"Patrick, are you sure McDermott is waiting until this afternoon to set the explosives?"

"Yes, he can't do it too far in advance or the linemen might notice something and telegraph a warning. The man who met us in Port Carbon was not even moving the powder box until this morning."

"Who'll be guarding it?"

"McDermott scheduled men he trusts."

"Our timing is critical once we reach Tremont. It wouldn't do for someone to discover our deception too soon." I sighed. Locating Con in the crowd and laying out a convincing argument was the most precarious part of my scheme.

The haze cleared by the time we descended Fountain Mountain, and we reached the outskirts of Tremont with three hours to spare. Patrick concealed the wagon in a thick patch of blazing red sumacs and paid a young lad playing near Railroad Street to care for the unhitched horses. We scuttled down one of the rocky trails that led from the road to the railbed below. The earthy smell of crushed mushrooms and ferns mixed with the sharp scent of coal tar from the railroad ties as we reached the level. Once in the open we saw the milling crowd a half mile down the tracks and started toward them.

"Hello, Patrick. Dominick." One of McDermott's men that we met in Audenreid greeted us as we mingled.

"These folks are from up the line in Hazleton." He introduced us to the group, but after a few remarks the men went back to talking with their friends.

Newcomers who arrived on foot sat on a leaf-covered slope sharing lunchpails of bread, cheese, and apples. Groups of men and boys in dirty work clothes continued to arrive from the collieries in Cass township. McDermott's men had hauled hundreds of them from Heckscher's mines. Standing out among the miners were bearded German farmers in straw hats, their trousers held up with braces. A lump formed in my throat at the sight of the crowd.

"Pat, this group is five times the size I expected."

"Should we abandon our plans?"

"Lordy, no! Oh, I don't know." I swallowed hard, then scanned the scene to weigh our chances.

Only a few men carried arms, but many had cudgels or

billies. A large group gathered around a barrel of liquid courage. I wondered if they would be able to put McDermott's orders into effect since some were becoming tipsy, and they had several hours' wait.

McDermott, of course, was armed and busy moving from cluster to cluster, rallying the men.

"Remember, justice is on our side. Help any man who has been drafted against his will. Use any means possible to stop anyone who interferes."

His passion for the cause was obvious, and I could see the powerful effect his presence had on the desperate miners. We would have to keep to our original plan.

"Pat, go see if you can locate where McDermott stashed the powder box. I'll look for Con."

I wended my way through the crowd, noting horses, wagons, and even a railroad handcar set for the escape. Leaders from the various castles of the Knights of the Golden Circle shouted slogans which echoed through the throng. "Fight to the death before fighting for Lincoln." "Come on, Irishmen! Come on, Dutchmen!"

The protest united those they called Buckshots or Mollies, with businessmen from the Golden Circle, miners, and farmers, people who in ordinary times stayed apart. The largest knot of men stood listening to speakers standing on a rocky outcrop addressing the crowd on a single theme. "If we stick together, they can't force us to go to war."

As I peered through the crowd milling at the foot of the hill, my heart jumped as I spied the familiar profile of Con Gallagher. Beside him stood Big Joe McDermott.

CHAPTER 19

Convincing Con

I glanced around for Pat. He had been gone for some time. I hoped he managed to move the box we brought from Hazleton to a location closer to the tracks.

My job was to separate Con from McDermott, and disclose my real identity. I mentally rehearsed how I would convince Con to disperse the crowd and find a better way to fight the injustice of the draft.

I whirled around when I heard heavy footsteps crunching behind me.

"Whisst! Patrick, thank goodness!"

"The switch is made." Coal dust packed in an identical box now replaced the black powder. "I dumped the explosives into Rausch Creek."

Now, for better or worse, we had to go forward with our plan.

"Were you seen?" I asked.

"I think everything went well enough. Harry McGee was guarding the powder and I sent him off to get lunch. He assumed I was his replacement. Half an hour later, when the real guard came on duty, he frowned when I got up to greet him, but didn't question me."

"I found Con. He's over there." I tilted my head to the left.

"If you can convince McDermott to address the crowd, I'll pull Con aside."

"I'll do my best," he said.

I edged to the side of the crowd where Con was standing. Moments later I saw Patrick hail McDermott. They stood watching the speaker who had switched from English to German. I saw Pat lean over and speak to Big Joe, who nodded in agreement. A few moments later McDermott made his way to the speaker's boulder. The crowd silenced as the Big Man composed himself to speak.

"In less than an hour the mine owners, Bannan, Tower, and men of their ilk will understand our position against this blasted war." His speech was as fiery and persuasive as any I'd ever heard from a lectern or pulpit.

"Remember Keenan and McAloon. Is the army taking care of their widows and children? What about Mrs. McHale who will have no one to care for her in her old age if Thady is killed in this unnecessary fight? What'll your children do if you're drafted?" Murmurs from the crowd revealed their oneness of opinion.

McDermott saw a familiar face and called, "Mulhern, who collected the $300 fee so you could pay the commissioner and stay here where you're needed?"

"That would be yourself, Joe!" shouted Mulhern.

McDermott's glib tongue and confident air would lure the wrens from the hedges, but to me he was a dangerous enemy. My time to move was now, while the crowd was totally enthralled. I took a deep breath and approached Con where he stood next to Patrick. I jostled his shoulder and looked straight into his eyes as he turned to face me. His eyes narrowed in thought as he scanned my features, then widened in recognition. His dark brows lowered.

Without a word I nudged Con beyond the edge of the crowd toward the German farmers. He barely waited to be apart from the group before exclaiming, "My God, what are you doing here?"

"I'm here to save your neck and to get you to help me disperse this mob."

"Have you gone mad? No one on Earth can stop things now."

"Then more innocent people will die. Please talk to them. These bright and passionate men can end this war and move up in the world, but violence isn't the way."

"Bannan and Tower don't understand anything except violence so we're doing things the way they understand!" said Con.

"You're single, but many of these men have wives and children depending on them."

"They're here of their own free will, Katie."

"Maybe or maybe not, but one thing is sure, they're to be the ones to change the fate of the Irish who come after us. Don't squander them. Too many have already been tossed away like kindling for this war."

My voice hitched to a stop as I thought about Con's cousin John and the other boys I knew who had died. Con stared into my eyes and seemed to read my thoughts, then looked down.

"I've had plenty of time to think of our losses. McDermott's message made sense, and he helped me after Dinny's accident. I felt like I was drowning, and he threw me a line. Even if I'm not so sure now, we've gone too far to halt."

"You have to stop them, Con." I spoke in a flat, emphatic tone. Con stared into my face for clues.

"What do you mean?"

"You're putting your family in danger. Even if you no longer care about yourself, consider your grandmother, your mother, and Dinny."

"You're just trying to sway me by saying that I'm endangering them."

"I have proof." I pulled out Pardee's letter and gave it to Con.

He frowned as he read, then glanced up. I explained how I had eavesdropped and exchanged the letter. The serious look on his face gave me hope, as did his first words.

"How can we keep McDermott from blowing up the tracks?"

"He doesn't have any blasting powder."

"What do you mean? Of course he has powder. McDermott told the Heckschersville men to swarm the tracks as soon as they saw the signal that the fuse was lit."

"Oh my God! They'll all be killed when the train doesn't derail."

Con grabbed my shoulders and shook me. "What haven't you told me?"

"Th- the box..."

I covered my eyes with trembling palms, horrified by visions of the train barreling into the assembled protesters. I should have asked for help from the authorities instead of interfering on my own. Now I'd be responsible for a terrible tragedy!

"My plan was to exchange coal dust for the powder today, when it was too late to get more. Patrick made the switch an hour ago. No one knows except the three of us."

CHAPTER 20

Climax

Tears pricked beneath my eyelids.

"Katie, you have no time for remorse. Find Pat, and meet me back here. I'll need help to rig up a plan." My spine stiffened at Con's stern command.

I pivoted into the crowd, hoping Pat was still there. We must stop the men from storming the tracks. With the train speeding down the mountain, many could be killed. Where was Pat?

"Dominick!" My stomach jumped, and my heart thumped wildly. Oh Lordy, it's Felty! I wanted to bolt into the crowd, but it was too late to avoid him.

Felty closed in. "How'd you get here?" Didn't see you with the gang from McGinty's."

"I came with Patrick. Have you seen him?"

"He was with Big Joe. They went off in that direction." He pointed. "C'mon, I'm goin' that way."

I had to shuck off Felty before talking to Pat, but he stuck to me like a burr on a collie's tail. Thoughts writhed and pounded in my head. I was ready to scream in frustration when Felty said, "Ah, there they are!"

I reached the group surrounding Big Joe McDermott and nudged Pat. "I ran into a lad I grew up with in Allentown. I'd like you to meet him." Pat's open face showed that he had not picked up on my meaning.

"Joe was just telling us the plans for the train. I'll stay and listen a while," he said.

I tapped my foot and sucked in a deep breath. Time was ticking away toward tragedy. Now what? Being in McDermott's company was more than I could bear.

"Patrick, I'll see you back at the rock when you finish. I'll be with my old friend, and I'd really like to introduce you to him."

Pat's eyes flickered in understanding at the words "old friend," but he had to remain with Joe until the discussion was over. My only consolation was that Felty also stayed.

Arrivals to the site had slowed, but the crowd on the railbed was considerable. Once in place, the multitude would never get off the tracks in time. Crushing guilt restricted my breathing when I imagined the men trampling each other to jump out of the locomotive's path. I shook my head to banish the image and returned to the speaker's rock.

Con had sketched out a scheme while I was gone. Several miners huddled near him, listening.

"We'll tell the guard that McDermott wants him to check the powder. Once McDermott learns of the problem, he'll warn the men of a change of plans," said Con.

"Thank God!" My confidence returned.

"Where's your friend?" asked Con.

"He's with Big Joe, Felty, and some others talking over the original plan.

"Sam..., Jack..., you two go to the powder cache and tell the guard on duty that you suspect intrigue. Make him open the box in your sight and examine it. When he realizes it's only coal dust, he'll raise the alarm."

Con turned toward me. "Get Patrick and hightail it out of here while things are in chaos. When Joe interviews the guards, he'll realize you were likely the ones who made the swap. You'll be shot as traitors to the cause."

"I'm afraid for Patrick. No one here knows my real identity, but Pat's in jeopardy. He hasn't been disguised. Even if the men on duty don't know his name, they can easily describe him. McDermott will immediately know who the red-haired man in the groom's clothing was."

"Take him to the Patch. See if he can stay with someone trustworthy in the community. If that doesn't work, ask for sanctuary from Father Maloney."

"I'll manage somehow." I spoke with more conviction than I felt. "Pat and I can never go back to Pardee Square, but we'll have to arrange for the horses and wagon to be returned so the sheriff isn't called."

"I'll send word to Pardee Square saying that you eloped with Patrick. Otherwise, they'll send out a search party. James, my friend from Audenreid, takes my pay to the Patch every week. He can drive the wagon back and tell your employers that you ran off with Pat."

"Where'll you go, Con?"

"My plans were to go with McDermott, but I'll have to change them after this. No one will be above suspicion."

"Tell your men to wait until Pat has left McDermott's side before approaching the powder cache."

Waiting until Pat joined me was torture. Time was ticking away, and a few more precious minutes were lost explaining the terrifying situation to Patrick.

"We'll join the crowd and be prepared to escape in the confusion of the upcoming announcement. When Joe announces that the powder is missing, there will be a surge of confusion that will help us to escape."

"God, Katie, McDermott's a madman. I thought we'd be far away from here before he discovered his plan was ruined," said Patrick.

Con walked over to McDermott. Minutes later, the guard on powder duty shouted for Joe to come quick. Con returned to me and waited to approach Joe about informing the crowd.

McDermott came back down to the level raging,. "Sons of bitches! Traitors stole the powder I know was in that box."

Patrick nudged me and murmured, "Let's get out of here."

We watched in growing fear as Joe McDermott continued to rant. "I'll shoot the bastards who did this. Our men will be killed on the tracks, making the thieves black-hearted murderers."

"Surely you won't send the men onto the tracks now!" said Con. The look of shock on his face was replaced by disgust. "If the train isn't derailed by an explosion, it'll have a full head of steam..."

"Stopping the train is our goal. The men who die will be martyrs for the cause."

"No Joe, the reason we're here is to save lives and prevent children from becoming orphans."

"We have to oppose the leaders forcing us to fight their battles. Any losses are casualties of war, Con."

"Joe, I've followed you at risk of my skin, but I can't allow this. The men must be informed. If you won't do it, I will."

Joe's eyes shone with a murderous light. He lunged forward to grab Con, but Con had already bounded toward the speaker's stand.

Men gathered as rumor of an important announcement spread. Con commanded the crowd's attention very quickly.

His address was short but powerful. "Today we planned to derail the train and rush the tracks. We wanted to help the consignees escape. Somebody disrupted that plan by taking the blasting powder."

Angry comments erupted from the crowd.

"We can still make our stand!" someone yelled.

"The train may not stop or even slow down for men lined

up on the tracks. You have a chance to leave now, if that be your choice," said Con.

Murmurs rose in volume like a rain of coal tumbling down a chute, starting with a few trickles and increasing to a near roar. Con's announcement incited a mixed reaction.

A man near me said, "I'm staying."

But his companion disagreed. "What's the use of being docked a day's pay if nothing happens?"

Another responded, "I'm leaving, too. I'll join Tinker Ward and the peaceful protesters.

"Yeh, there's no difference between dyin' in this fight and dyin' in battle. Dead is dead!" The two men left their companion and headed up the path that led away from the tracks. German farmers on the far side of the crowd were also disbanding.

McDermott warned Con to jump down, but Con ignored him and continued answering questions. Confused listeners swarmed him for more information when he left off speaking.

When McDermott took the speaker's role, he had a smaller audience. Clusters of grim-faced men trudged up the slope to the road, but McDermott performed his word-magic on the undecided. The remaining group split, with the larger number staying.

"Pat, you must get away before Joe starts interrogating people."

"I'm ready to go back to Hazleton. We've done our bit," said Pat.

"We can't return to Pardee Square! You have to hide out where no one knows you."

To my mind, the Patch was the only place safe enough.

"Con, what about you? McDermott won't take your position kindly. After your speech, he may even suspect you of the powder theft."

"He may tag me as a conspirator, but he knows I didn't have time to steal the powder. He'll certainly be in a dangerous mood though."

"Where will you go after all this?"

"I can't stay around here, but I don't have enough money to go west to California. I'll go as far as my fare will take me."

A faint echoing whistle sounded as the train rounded the bend at Newtown, just north of Tremont. No time now to do more, but at least the men knew the risk.

"Pat, go hitch the horses," said Con. "You have to leave before word of the train stoppage gets out. Troops will arrive as soon as they hear."

Pat left quickly as the situation intensified.

Men tied handkerchiefs to their billies and waved them as they got into position on the tracks. McDermott positioned the handful of men with firearms near the front. Warning shots would be fired first, but if necessary, they would use the guns against any soldiers who resisted.

"Time to go, Katie. I'll see you at home before I leave the coal region."

"Send word as soon as you get to the Patch." I took off my scarf and tied it to the thick walking stick I carried. "Here, may it bring you luck, my friend."

Con's lips tilted in a crooked smile as he accepted it. His eyes expressed unspoken feelings. He nodded, patted my shoulder, and joined the men on the tracks. My last glimpse was the fringe of my scarf fluttering over Con's coal black hair.

I sighed and hiked up the path to Railroad Street where Pat left the wagon.

"Come on, Katie! The word is out about the plan. The troops will be here any time now!" Patrick's face was flushed. "There's nothing left for you to do."

I glanced back down at the scene, torn between getting Patrick to safety and staying with Con. The task we set for ourselves was done, but the outcome was still hanging in the balance. Pat reached down and hoisted me into the wagon, then directed the well-rested horses north.

We had only traveled part way up the mountain road when one of the wagon wheels began to wobble. "Och, the horses are fresh, but now this! All the luck I have is bad," Patrick growled.

We pulled over in a clearing when the jarring worsened. I got out and wandered off to find a pond or stream while Pat took out tools to make repairs. I had not gone far when my exploration was halted by a sudden drop-off.

Looking down the ravine, I had a clear view of the miles of railroad track between McDermott's men and the locomotive. The black engine of my fears was a distant speck to the north, but the men below were surprisingly clear, though south of the bluff where I stood. The twisting road Pat and I traveled had not taken us very far as the crow flies.

I scanned the rocky terrain and spotted a whitetail doe part way down the steep cliff. As I watched her nibble at shrubs, an idea came to me, and I paced along the edge, squinting my eyes against the bright sunlight.

My heart leaped when I spotted a bare place that marked a pathway blazed by foraging animals. I skittered down the slope with my fingers crossed, hoping the trail went all the way down the notch.

Small rocks and clumps of crumbling clay bounced ahead of me, spooking the deer. My spirits deflated as I watched the doe scamper farther along the path. The trail circled back up the embankment instead of zigzagging down to the bottom.

I flopped down on a boulder. My eyes burned with unshed tears, and I flung a handful of pebbles down the slope in frustration. If only I could get down there.

"Katie, KATIE!" Patrick's desperate tone jolted me from my thoughts. I picked my way back up to the clearing. He met me at the head of the trail, face crinkled with concern. "I thought you fell off the cliff!"

"I'm sorry, Pat."

"What in the world were you doing down there?"

"I had a plan to pile shrubs and rocks on the tracks to stop the train, but the path doesn't reach the railbed."

Pat looked down the embankment then stared off in thought. When he glanced back at me I saw his eyes light up. "Wait! You wouldn't need to go all the way down!" He was pacing along the edge. "One of those boulders rolling down the cliff would block the tracks. We'll have to hurry though." He ran back to the wagon as I looked at the boulders.

Pat came back with the lever he had used on the wheel. "C'mon Katie, let's finish our mission!" We headed down the narrow path as quickly as safety allowed.

I pointed out an area of loose scrabble topped by a sizable rock. "If we can loosen the smaller rocks, this one will move."

We kicked out most of the loose stone around the boulder, then Pat wedged the lever into the ground behind the huge chunk of granite. Pat pushed down on the lever while I planted a foot to push against the rock, clinging to a shrub for balance.

"Heave!" directed Patrick, and we combined our strength to push. Three times he gave the order before we felt a slight give. The small result drove us to work harder. Pat's face turned reddish-purple, and my arm and leg muscles trembled in our next effort, but we were rewarded by more success. The boulder rolled part way out of its cradle of earth. Only two more shoves and it was tumbling down the hillside, causing a dusty avalanche of debris.

When the air cleared, I saw that we were more successful than I had dreamed possible. A mound of fallen rock covered the rails. I swiped my sleeve across my brow and grinned at Pat. "That was a fine plan. I didn't know you had it in you!"

"Here they come!" The men on the tracks were marching around the bend. From the trail, we also had a view of the train's deadly progress. My heart thumped, and I closed my eyes. I prayed that the locomotive would stop short of the crowd.

My eyes popped open at the screech of train brakes. The

huge black monster came to a shuddering halt mere yards from the rock fall, then chaos erupted.

Rioters waved their billies and ran toward the train, surrounding it. The crew shouted directions as shaken passengers poured out of the cars. Soldiers herded the draftees into a rough circle, but they were outmanned by McDermott's gang and were forced to release the men after a brief fight. A few went down, but I could not tell if anyone was seriously injured.

I searched the mass of churning people for Con. My heart leaped as I spotted my scarf dangling from the cudgel. He was in the thick of things, helping a woman with three children who were caught in the clash. I saw him hoist a young boy onto his shoulder as he led the woman and her other children away from the confusion. Thank God he was safe!

"Let's go, Katie! Nothing more we can do here." Pat reverted to his familiar worrywart personality.

"Is the wheel fixed?" In all the excitement, I almost forgot the reason we stopped.

"Yes. Now we have to get away. Troops will block off this area."

I dragged my gaze from the scene and looked down at my disguise. "I need to change before we get to the Patch." I climbed onto the bench of the wagon. "There wasn't any water here."

"I think there's a spring up ahead," said Pat.

We traveled a short distance to a secluded area near a stream where I washed my face, braided my hair, and changed into a gown. Though I worked quickly, as soon as we returned to the road we heard pounding hoofbeats.

A regiment of soldiers blasted past us on the road with barely a glance. The telegraph office at Tremont must have transmitted the news to Pottsville moments after the train was stopped.

Patrick practiced the story he would tell once we got to the Patch. Hiding him from the authorities would require help. I would ask Breslin if he could stay at his house. No one else who had room could be trusted.

When we pulled up at Grandmam's house, Maymie came out on the porch to see who had arrived. She stared a moment, then ran back inside to tell everyone. My family was stunned to see me, but surprise quickly changed to hugs and tears of joy. I ushered Patrick in and explained the situation, anxious to get messages out to Breslin and the Gallaghers.

A sharp knock startled all of us. Aunt Aggie whisked Patrick into the parlor. I held my breath as Grammam opened the door.

"Deirdre!" Con's mother came in carrying a basket of herbs. Relieved, I ran forward and hugged her. We brought Patrick back into the kitchen and introduced him.

"Con was with us at the train riot this afternoon," I said.

Deirdre clutched the neckline of her shawl with a shaking hand and placed her basket on the table. "Was he hurt?"

"He wasn't when we saw him last." I explained the situation and told Deirdre that Con's instructions were to hide Pat and send the wagon back to Pardee Square. "Con expects to return home tonight, if all goes well."

Deirdre quietly accepted the news, then bustled off to ask Breslin and his sister if they would make room for an unexpected guest.

CHAPTER 21

Concealment – October 17, 1862

"No word from Con yet." Deirdre bent over her well-scrubbed kitchen table pouring tea. Dinny, Old Missus Gallagher, Mother, Sarah and I clutched our mugs, listening to her news. "Pat is settled in at Breslin's. Ellen put out the story that their nephew arrived for a visit on the way to Philadelphia to start a new job. Breslin actually did get your friend a position with Goosey McHugh, a blacksmith down in Chester. He's taking Pat to meet the Mauch Chunk train tomorrow."

"Thank God things are working out. I embroiled poor Patrick in all this against his will, and I'd be devastated if something happened to him. What other rumors are out there?" I asked.

"Everyone is talking about yesterday's events, both at Pottsville station and south on the tracks. Four men were shot in the donnybrook at Tremont," said Deirdre.

"Were they killed or wounded?"

"No one knows, but eighteen were arrested and taken to the county jail at Pottsville."

"They say Joe McDermott escaped arrest, but soldiers apprehended a dozen of his men," said Mother.

"The poor fools! Joe beguiled them with his hot words and

then led them to the slaughter, not caring about the consequences. Thanks goodness more were not killed." said Old Mrs. Gallagher.

I shuddered imagining the protesting mass of miners being gutted by the racing train. I could not regret stopping the train when so many lives had been at risk.

"Tinker Ward and several other nonviolent demonstrators were among the men arrested, even though they had not been involved in anything illegal. They had been at the Pottsville station protesting peacefully during the riot near Tremont."

My heart sank when I heard that news. Those men had sought to avoid hostility, but they were made scapegoats by the angry authorities. Calm reasoning had not saved them.

Footsteps pattering across the porch and a quick knock announced Winnie's arrival. She rushed in with the Pottsville newspaper. The headlines were all about yesterday's events. Bannan's reports in the paper were extremely hostile. He called for Federal troops to be sent to Pottsville to control the coal fields.

It sounded like Benjamin Bannan now hated Irish Catholic Democrats more than ever. He had made a fool of himself in the eyes of Governor Curtin and Secretary of War Stanton by greatly exaggerating the force and fire power of the protesters, and he would never forgive the Irish for his loss of face.

While certain details of the unfortunate events were sketchy, of one thing I was certain. Conflict had worsened in the coal region, and it was not something that would be easily forgotten.

When we returned home, Aunt Aggie brought word that Con had evaded the authorities, but suffered a broken arm in the fighting. "He's staying out of town until tomorrow and leaving for the west on the noon train from Pottsville. Deirdre is heartbroken, but she knows it is the only possible way to save him."

CHAPTER 22

Conclusion

Winnie hired a driver to take us to the Pottsville station. While Winnie paid the driver, I ran ahead to the departure platform. The train depot was more frenzied than usual since curiosity seekers gawked to see where the events of the previous afternoon unfolded.

I spotted Con leaning against the wall of the station with his jacket draped over his left arm. He straightened and approached when he saw me wave. His splinted and wrapped arm was held close to his body by the knit scarf I had given him in Tremont.

"Katie. Thank God you're alright!"

"What about you?" I asked, glancing at the injured arm.

"I'm fine," he said shortly. "For safety's sake, don't ask about yesterday," muttered Con.

While waiting for Winnie, I asked Con some of the questions that had nagged at me for the past weeks.

"How did you recognize me that night at Bach's Hotel in Audenreid?" Con smiled wryly and said, "By scent!"

He laughed outright at my surprised face and explained. "You were wearing my grandmother's famous cold cream. Haven't I helped with that recipe since I was a lad? As soon as I caught a whiff of cucumber, I thought of the Patch. Once my suspicions were stirred, the pieces of the puzzle came together."

"Why didn't you tell me?"

"I couldn't speak to you that night, of course. I decided to frighten you off anonymously. That's why I paid young Seamus to deliver the warnings to Pardee Square. I thought the left-handed, misspelled notes would put you off, but I should have known you'd be too stubborn to heed them. My blood ran cold when I saw you yesterday."

"Katie!"

I turned to see Wynnie rushing down the platform as the passengers began to board the train. She brought the money she and Jill had saved from their employment. Con stuck out his unslung hand to shake Wynnie's in embarrassed thanks at taking charity from a woman, but Wynnie gingerly pulled him forward in a brief and cautious hug.

"You're kind beyond my dreams, Wynnie, I'll repay you once I get on my feet in Wisconsin," said Con.

"You've had a bad time of it this year, Con. I only pray that no other misfortune befalls you," said Wynnie.

"If I don't get out of here now, I'll be trapped between the authorities and the remnants of McDermott's gang.

Con turned to me and said, "I'm grateful, plain and sure, that you brought me to my senses before it was too late."

"Don't worry about thanking me. Your mother and grandma did so much for my family over the years. It's merely just compensation I'm giving," I said.

Someone in the crowd hailed Wynnie, and she moved away, allowing us more time alone.

"I'll be known as Dan Connor when I get off in Erin Prairie. I'm changing my name for the sake of my skin, just in case anyone tracks me to Wisconsin." He cocked his head and smiled ruefully. "Take care of yourself, lass. It'd be best if you shook the dust of the region from your feet, too." Con paused and grasped my hand. "Will you not come with me?"

My heart wrenched at his words, but I looked him in the eye and shook my head. I gave his hand a final squeeze, then released it. "Wynnie and I are planning to leave for New York once we hear from Mrs. Evans's friend. There are many opportunities in the city."

"So our Wynnie is finally going to get the chance to write music and play professionally!" Con's heartiness struck a false note, but I was relieved he accepted my decision without fuss.

"Yes, and I'll work in service at one of the big houses. Once I earn enough, I'll start an employment agency for immigrant girls. They need decent wages and better working conditions."

The mournful train whistle sounded, reminding us that our time to say farewell was short. Our childhood friendship was ending with Con's departure.

"Good-bye, Katie. For now at least."

"Call me Kate. I'm due for a name change, too. I don't feel like a Katie anymore. Those days are behind me, along with the youthful fancies I had two years ago." I hugged my old friend and swallowed the burning pain that choked my voice.

The conductor yelled, "All aboard! Final call!" Wynnie scurried back to the platform.

Con tossed his satchel onto the train, grabbed the railing with his good arm, and jumped up the two steps as the train coasted down the tracks. Wynnie and I waved until the train's outline was lost in the spewing dust and cinders.

∽ The End ∽

LITERATURE CIRCLE QUESTIONS

❧ ❧

The questions and activities below complement the reading of *Call Me Kate: Meeting the Molly Maguires.* They are designed to tap the levels of learning measured on open-ended assessments.

1. Describe the McCaffertys' lives before and after the mine accident. How did their lives change?

2. What does Katie believe is the reason for Mr. Breslin's visit in chapter two? Was her incorrect conclusion realistic under the circumstances? Explain why or why not.

3. Which events show that Katie is close to her family even if they sometimes disagree? Does this seem realistic?

4. Describe the society of the mining patch. How does it differ from society today?

5. How does Katie feel about leaving school before getting her diploma? Compare her feelings to those of her parents. According to her father, what is the importance of education?

6. Conflict and compromise are themes of this novel. Explain the reasons for the conflicts and both the positive and negative ways in which they were settled.

7. The Civil War was the bloodiest conflict in our country's history. How did Katie feel about the war and her country at the beginning of the novel? Did her feelings change? If so, how?

8. Which groups in the North were antiwar protesters? Explain each group's perspective.

9. Katie has both old and new friends in *Call Me Kate*. List the qualities that embody a good friend. Which of these characteristics are exhibited by characters in the novel?

10. Compare Kate to another character in literature or to someone you know personally. Explain the similarities and differences.

EXTENSION ACTIVITIES

A. Draw a map showing Murphy's Patch in relation to Pottsville, Hazleton, and Tremont. Indicate mountains, railroads, and rivers. Show the distance between each area.

B. Create a model railroad scene for display (e.g., leaving the Mauch Chunk station for Hazleton.)

C. Research the Molly Maguires. Did the group actually exist? Discuss your opinion in an essay.

GLOSSARY OF TERMS

෯ ৯

banshee:	a female witch whose piercing wail foretold a death, especially the death of a member of certain old Irish families
Black Mariah:	a black carriage used to transport injured or dead miners
blatherskite:	a talkative person, full of foolishness or nonsense
breaker boy:	person who removes the slate from the coal in the breaker; a job usually held by the very young or very old
brogans:	ankle high, sturdy leather shoes
buttie/butty:	miner's young helper or workmate
changeling:	in Irish mythology, one of the "little people" who may replace a human infant in the cradle if the parents were not careful
clinker:	lumpy reddish rock found near coal deposits, formed from unburned coal
colliery:	the entire coal mine operation, including the office, breaker, wash house, shaft, and out buildings
corpse house:	any house where a wake takes place
cribbing:	the beams holding up the roof of the mine

culm bank:	waste anthracite coal, slate, and dirt piled up outside the colliery
donnybrook:	a rough, noisy fight; named after Donnybrook Fair in Dublin, Ireland
dooley box:	a sturdy box used to pack Dualite dynamite made by the DuPont Co.; Families took the boxes for many uses since they were very well made.
feckless:	irresponsible, incompetent
fire boss:	a section foreman who lit the dynamite when blasting; a responsible and relatively well-paid position
firedamp:	explosive gas found in coal mines, made up of methane mixed with other gases
gingham:	lightweight woven cotton or linen fabric, often in a checked pattern
gob:	a mix of dirt, slate and waste left over from mining
gulder:	a boisterous shout or laugh
hooligan:	wild, rowdy person
laudanum:	opiate used in the nineteenth century to relieve pain
macushla:	Irish meaning "my darling"
night rail:	bed clothes, night shirt

nipper:	young boy who worked inside the mines in a dangerous job, opening and closing the doors for the mule-driven carts of coal
Old Nick:	name used for the devil
Old Sod:	nickname for Ireland, the old country
patch:	a small village of company-owned homes built near the mines
poteen:	homemade whiskey
tweeny:	a "between maid;" one of the lower members in the servant hierarchy

REFERENCES

Bartoletti, *Susan C. Black Potatoes: The Story of the Great Irish Famine, 1845 to 1850.* New York: Houghton Mifflin, 2001.

Bartoletti, Susan C. *A Coal Miner's Bride: The Diary of Anetka Kaminska, 1896.* New York: Scholastic, 2000.

Campbell, Patrick. *A Molly Maguire Story.* Jersey City, NJ: P.H. Campbell, 1992.

Coffey, Michael, ed. *The Irish in America.* New York: Hyperion, 1997.

Crown, H.T. *A Molly Maguire on Trial: The Thomas Munley Story.* Frackville, PA: Broad Mountain Publishing, 2002.

Davies, Edward J. *The Anthracite Aristocracy: Leadership and Social Change in the Hard Coal Regions of Northeastern Pennsylvania, 1800-1930.* DeKalb, IL: Northern Illinois University Press, 1985.

Delaney, Mary M. *Of Irish Ways.* New York: Harper and Row, 1973.

Hughes, Pat. *The Breaker Boys.* New York: Farrar, Straus & Giroux, 2004.

Kenny, Kevin. *Making Sense of the Molly Maguires.* New York: Oxford University, 1998.

Long, E.B., and Barbara Long. *The Civil War Day by Day: An Almanac 1861-1865.* New York: Da Capo, 1971.

Miller, Kerby, and Patricia M. Miller. *A Journey of Hope: the Story of Irish Immigration to America.* San Francisco: Chronicle, 2001.

Moloney, Mick. *Far from the Shamrock Shore: The Story of Irish-American Immigration through Song.* New York: Crown, 2002.

Palladino, Grace. *Another Civil War: Labor, Capital, and the State in the Anthracite Regions of Pennsylvania 1840-68.* New York: Fordham University Press, 2006.

Wallace, Anthony F.C. *St. Clair: A Nineteenth Century Coal Town's Experience with a Disaster Prone Industry.* Ithaca, NY: Cornell University Press, 1987.

Ward, Leo. "It was Open Defiant Rebellion." *Civil War,* 9.2, (1991): 56-63.

ACKNOWLEDGMENTS

I gratefully acknowledge the support and encouragement of many generous people who helped me bring my dream of authorship to fruition. First, I must recognize Hildy Morgan and the Endless Mountain Writers group at the Dietrich Theater in Tunkhannock. The critiques offered every Thursday night are invaluable. Thanks, gang!

Sincere thanks to Howard T. Crown, author and guide extraordinaire, who readily answered my many questions about the Molly Maguires during our eight hour tour. Without his help this book would not exist.

My gratitude also to Stu Richards, Tom Dempsey, and the helpful staff of the Schuylkill County Historical Society who graciously answered my questions about Schuylkill County and Civil War history.

My appreciation is also extended to the Yahoo online interest groups dedicated to the Molly Maguires, the coal region, and northeast Pennsylvania ancestors. The boards have been a treasure trove of information.

To my son, John Garrett Slaby, who expended his time and talent to capture Katie's image in paint, kudos.

Thank you to the meticulous Bill Chapla who read my work in progress and made editorial suggestions to improve my manuscript.

Any errors in *Call Me Kate*, whether factual, grammatical, or mechanical are mine and not the responsibility of any of my contributors.

And finally, posthumous thanks to my great-great grandmother, Catharine McCafferty Boyle Gallagher, whose real life was almost as dramatic as the fictional Kate's.

LaVergne, TN USA
23 August 2009
155667LV00005B/9/P